The Path's End

An Ed and Mel Decodable Adventure

Heather Doolittle

The characters and events in this book are fictitious. Any similarity to real persons, living or dead, or actual events is purely coincidental and not intended by the author.

DecodableAdventures.com

ISBN-13: 979-8-6889-7917-6

To the Weavers,
who have encouraged me countless times over the years,
and to
Michael Pyle
It has meant a lot to me to collaborate with you
on these Ed and Mel books.
Thanks for everything.

Forward

As I finish up writing the Ed and Mel's Decodable Adventures trilogy, I realize how much of my family's journey with dyslexia has ended up on the pages. There have been highs, and there have been lows. Weaknesses threatened to derail futures while strengths, encouragement, and community brought hope. As we continued down our path, there was something else as well. We got to a point where we found our stride. We were able to accept weaknesses, comfortably use tools such as assistive technology, and lean into strengths and interests. We were able to look back at old trials and see how the lessons learned were helping with today. We have much more traveling to do, but the journey to acceptance feels like it is complete.

The Path's End finishes this part of Ed and Mel's story. In it, Ed and Mel finally come face to face with R. L. Nox. There are decisions that must be made and consequences that must be accepted.

The Path's End is designed to be read by the student AND the parent or tutor. The narrator passages are for the parent or tutor to read, the student will read the student text, and the games are for everyone to play.

Skills are added to the student text as the story progresses. The student text follows the Level 5 Barton Reading & Spelling scope and sequence closely. Notes will help the parent or tutor know which skills are being added to the student reading passage and game. Variations from the Barton scope and sequence are minor and will be noted. It can be read when a student has completed Barton Reading & Spelling Level 5, or portions of it can be read as the student progresses through Level 5. This book may also be used with other Orton-Gillingham inspired programs or phonics programs.

Also, as a chapter book, the only starting and stopping points are where a bookmark is placed. A bookmark is a great symbol of recognizing the need to end an activity with the anticipation of picking it up again at a later time. Have your student pick out a bookmark before starting *The Path's End*. It may be a great signal for your student to use to say, "I need a break. I will start again later."

I hope *The Path's End* is an encouragement to students as they practice their new skills and follow Ed and Mel's journey to stop R. L. Nox.

Chapter 1

Required skills for student text:

Ability to read plural words using s and es.

Sight words: hour, county, word, another, won, above, eye, out, house, month, laugh, answer, four, thought.

Barton Level: **Level 5 lesson 1**.

Note: The word "oh" is used out of order from the Barton scope and sequence.

Notes for the book:

There is an occasional use of apostrophe + s for a possessive noun. e.g. Jax's, Mel's.
The word "watch" is used out of order from the Barton scope and sequence.
When a word varies from the Barton scope and sequence it will be noted in the "Required skills" box and underlined in the text.

Narrator (Parent or Tutor):

Dear Reader,

Have you ever felt like you are missing something? Maybe you missed part of a conversation and don't know what your friends are talking about. Maybe you forgot your homework that is due at the beginning of the school day. Maybe you don't have an answer to a question about your reading passage. Maybe you are hunting down a greedy villain who keeps escaping all your efforts to catch him.

Ed Davis tossed and turned as he slept. His dreams were full of all the things he had missed as he, his twin sister Mel, and his Ebrinte friend Jax had been hunting after the villain R. L. Nox. First he dreamt of when his parents were kidnapped by R. L. They slept in the same room as him now, but Ed and his twin sister Mel had to follow The Black Silk Path through a magical doorway to Ebrin to find them. That was after they had to travel half-way across the world twice to even find The Black Silk Path.

Ed also dreamt about the spell R. L. had put on them. The spell took away their ability to speak, read, and write. Even in his dream, Ed knew he would wake up and still be under the spell. In his dream, the spell made it so that no sound came out of his mouth when tried to warn people of an ambush during a fierce battle. A stream of fire blasted over his head, causing him to hit the deck. He put his hands out to help push himself back up, but before he could stand, he felt the ground start to move. Large insects covered the ground and his hands. Ed jumped back, shaking his hands vigorously. The insects started to climb into a farmer's market stall and eat all the food it had for sale. A merchant walked up to him and asked, "Why don't you stop them? Maybe if you just tried harder." A nearby alligator spit out his coffee when he heard the comment and started laughing at Ed.

Ed awoke with a start. Sweat ran down his forehead, and he was out of breath. He must have awoken his mother, as she came over and sat next to him. She didn't say anything. She just put her arm around Ed. His mom knew how difficult this journey had been for him and Mel.

When R. L. Nox took Mom and Dad, Ed and Mel didn't know if they'd ever see them again. But somehow, step by step, Ed and Mel found a way to start breaking the power of the spell so they could find their parents. Each word Ed and Mel learned to read gave them a word they could speak. It wasn't easy to learn to read with the spell working against them, but they wouldn't give up. Ed and Mel's determination helped them to start speaking again. It helped them to follow the clues to find The Black Silk Path to get to Ebrin and rescue their parents. Now they were hunting the man responsible.

R. L. Nox had a master plan to steal as much of the riches of Ebrin as he could. When Ed and Mel saved their parents, they were able to warn the Ebrinites of his plan. Even though R. L.'s original plan was ruined, he was determined to get what he thought he deserved. He destroyed a town and a market in Ebrin, stealing everything he could. He didn't care about the mess he left behind or the people he hurt. He also stole two baby dragons, or Felkin, as the Ebrinites called them. R. L. took the dragons back to his world to put them in a circus. He figured people would pay a lot of money to see real dragons.

Speaking of missing something, there was some information that R. L. was missing. A toxin, introduced centuries ago, made it impossible for dragons to live for very long in Ed and Mel's world. The dragons had fled to different realms to escape the toxin. Ebrin became home for the Felkin dragons. Ebrin had the ingredients for a cure and became a place where they felt at home. Soon after, a few humans found a home in Ebrin as well. They lived together peacefully for generations.

When R. L. brought the baby dragons to his world, he exposed them to this toxin. If the babies died, the Felkin kind of Ebrin would not continue to the next generation. This would affect the whole ecosystem of Ebrin, as the Felkin tamed earthquakes through their gold mining activity. Their mining released built up gas pressure deep in the ground. If the Felkin didn't release the pressure, severe earthquakes would become a daily event and destroy the land. Ebrin would once again become inhospitable to humans.

The baby dragons needed saving. The fate of the Ebrin people was dependent on the Davises' knowledge of R. L. Nox to stop him and save the baby dragons.

Even as doubt and feelings of not being enough plagued his dreams, Ed Davis, his sister, Mel, and their friend Jax were not going to give up on the hunt for R. L. Nox. They were going to see this through to the end, no matter how it ended.

Student text:

Mel got up from her bed. She could see that Ed and Mom were up. Dad and Jax were still asleep. "Ed. Mom. Are you okay?" Mel did ask.

Ed said, "I can't sleep well. In my sleep, we couldn't say anything at all, and Mom and Dad were missing again. There were insects in the shops and so on."

"Yuck, the insects! I think I will always feel a bit of panic when I see big insects from now on," said Mel.

"I keep thinking of the baby dragons, so I can't sleep," Mel said. "We will find out today how to craft the meds they need.

Then, we can go get the stuff to craft the meds. I can't wait to go to rescue the baby dragons. When do you think we can begin?"

Mom said, "I think people will be up in about an hour. You two should try to get some extra rest. It is going to be a long day. You have to study the specs for the meds. If you aren't exact, it will fail. If you slip up, the toxic meds could . . . oh, just don't let the meds contact your skin."

"Ok, Mom. You know we will be prudent," Mel said, "but I don't think I can rest now. I think I will pray and then begin to get my things. I also want to see the small dragon, the one that was so sick. I thought she wasn't going to last, but she is on the mend. She will be well again in a few days. See you in a bit. I love you bunches, Mom. Hugs and kisses."

"I love you bunches too, Mel. Hugs and kisses," Mom said. "Ed, do you think you can get some extra rest?"

"No," Ed did reply. "I think I will fold boxes to put the tents in. The dragons don't need the people's help now. Most of the people will go back to the shops in Caltrez today. They are going to go help fix up their shops.

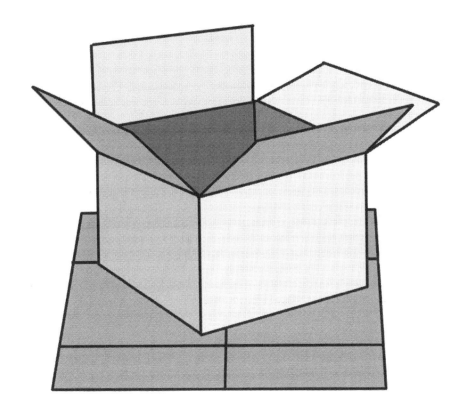

"Also, Mr. Maddox is going to brew some coffee for the people. I told him coffee is disgusting. He told me I hadn't had a sip of Ebrin coffee. Jax bet I will love Ebrin coffee. I bet that I still won't fancy it. Mr. Maddox wants to show me how he brews it and then let me try some."

Mom did grin. It was strange to think of Ed sipping coffee. It was amazing to <u>watch</u> her kids grow. Not long ago, Ed and Mel's job was to play, laugh, and munch their lunches. Now their "To Do" list had some big tasks:

1. Keep R. L. Nox away from Ebrin.
2. Find the components for the dragons' meds.
3. Craft the meds.
4. Find R. L. Nox and the baby dragons.
5. Rescue the dragons.
6. Stop R. L. You know, hero stuff.

They sure didn't let the spell R. L. put on them slow them up for long.

Game to play: Plural Paths

Every morning, Ed and Mel spend some time practicing their reading. Today they are working on the suffixes -s and -es by playing a game.

Materials needed:
- Game board and game cards. See Game Appendix.
- A game token for each player.

Rules:
1. Place the players' tokens at the "Start." There are two parallel paths. Each player will choose a path. A player must remain on the same path for the entire game unless they land on a space that allows them to change to the other path.
2. Player One draws a card and reads the word.
    a. If the word ends in "s", go to the next space with an "s." If the word ends in "es", go to the next space with an "es."
    b. If a player lands on a space with an arrow, they will move their token to the space to which the arrow points. Some arrows go back a space and some jump forward. If a player lands on a space with a double-sided arrow, they can choose to stay in the same spot or switch to the other path.
3. It is now Player Two's turn.
4. Reshuffle the cards as needed.
5. The first player to reach the end wins.

Chapter 2(a)

Additional required skills for student text:

Ability to read words with consonant suffixes such as -ly and -ness.

Barton Level: **Level 5 Lesson 2**.

Narrator (Parent or Tutor):

It was a beautiful morning. As the Ebrin sun came up, the hills and sky glowed in a thousand shades of green. Flowers in every color of the rainbow opened up on the hillsides as the sun hit their petals. The birds began to sing. Mel was getting used to hearing the songs of the unfamiliar birds. In fact, she looked forward to hearing them each morning. Their songs were an encouragement to her soul. The last few months had been difficult, but as Mel watched the Ebrinites wake up at the Felkin camp, she had a sense that all this difficulty was worth it. The dragon was right when it had given them advice. It was easy to think just about the difficulty and their failure to catch R. L. Nox. Mel had to let wisdom and thankfulness help her see the bigger picture more clearly. If R. L. hadn't kidnapped Mom and Dad, they wouldn't even know Ebrin existed. They would have never met Jax, Mr. Maddox, or their other new friends. They would have never seen a real dragon. They would have not known how determined they could be in fighting the spell. Now they did. And Mel was ready to use that determination to face the next obstacles that stood in their way.

Mel made her way over to Mr. Maddox's tent. She was just in time to see Ed's face wrinkle up as he stamped his foot and tried not to spill his drink. Apparently, Ed didn't like Ebrin coffee, either. Jax looked disappointed.

Student text:

"Don't fret, Jax," Mel said. "You successfully got Ed to sip coffee. That in itself is a win."

"I thought he would love it," Jax said. "I can't see why he doesn't. Most of the people in Ebrin drink it."

Ed cut in, "You should try some soda from my land. I feel sad for you if you think this drink is something to love."

"No sadness today!" Mel said. "I'll get a cup of coffee to try on our way to see Doc. This is the hour when we see how to protect the baby dragons." Mel had a sip of coffee and began to walk to Doc's tent.

Jax and Ed went with Mel to see Doc.

"Let me explain how to get all the elements to craft the meds," Doc said. "There are four things you must get. Two will be stress-free to get. They are plants you can find next to the paths and roads. Jax, you know the Ebrin Lily and the Indigo Bunch Grass plants." Jax did nod.

"The next one will be difficult to get," Doc did continue. "You must approach it thoughtfully. You need to get tree rat milk. Tree rats hang out in the tops of Laughfully Trees."

Jax did roll his eyes. "I know, Jax. It won't be a quick task," said Doc. "But you know it can be done."

Ed did ask, "Do the rats nip?"

"Only if you are a Laughfully Tree," Doc said. "It isn't risky to milk a tree rat. It is just difficult to catch them. You will have to ascend up to the top of a Laughfully Tree, wait for a rat to come next to you, and then quickly grab it. When you milk about twenty rats, you will have the milk you need plus a tiny bit extra.

"The last item you need is a very difficult one to get, but it is a critical component. You need to get a Shadow Jellyfish from Endless Bay."

Jax did not roll his eyes at this. In his

astonishment at what Doc said, he let out a gasp, shut his eyes, and almost sat on Ash.

The small ball of fluff ran to Mel. She pet Ash as she said, "Jax, are you okay?"

"Regretfully, I am not," Jax said. "It is madness to think we can just get a Shadow Jellyfish. We will need equipment. Then we will have to skillfully sail across the bay.

"When we find the exact spot, we will have to boldly swim below the smack of Shadow Jellyfish to skillfully grab one. If we mess up, the consequences are significant."

Mel said, "If we don't do anything, the consequences are significant. We have to do this, but we will do it as a band of friends. Thankfully, there *is* something that we can do to help the baby dragons. The spell R. L. put on us has had significant consequences, but we haven't let it stop us. We won't let a jellyfish stop us now."

Jax said, "Okay, we are not helpless.

This will be difficult, but we can find a way to do it."

"Mel," Doc said, "What Jax says is true, but I trust you all can do this. Let me tell you the details on how to craft the meds. You have to respect the process and the meds. If you don't get it exactly exact . . . yes, exactness is vital . . . you will fail.

"Also, you can't let it get on your skin. What rescues the dragons from a toxin is a toxin for you. Recklessness with it will end your quest. You must retain all of this info. Study it well."

Game to play: Avoid the Coffee

Mel liked the Ebrin coffee, but Ed sure didn't. Every time he saw someone with a cup of Ebrin coffee that morning, he got a sick feeling in his stomach. Watch out for the coffee cards in this game. They may give you a sick feeling in your stomach as well.

Materials needed:
- Game cards. See Game Appendix.

Rules:
1. Shuffle the cards and place them in one draw pile, face down.
2. Player One turns a card over and places it face up in a pile next to the draw pile. Player One reads the card and then decides if they want to draw another card. They can keep drawing cards until:
   a. They choose to stop and gain a point for each card they read or
   b. They draw a card with a picture of coffee. All the points gained on the turn must be given to the other player.
3. It is now Player Two's turn.
4. Play until all the cards have been played from the draw pile. The player who has the most points wins the game.

Chapter 2(b)

Additional required skills for student text:

Ability to read words with consonant suffixes such as -ly and -ness.

Barton Level: **Level 5 Lesson 2**.

Note: The word "worth" is used out of order from the Barton scope and sequence.

Narrator (Parent or Tutor):

Ed and Jax helped Mel study the medication directions for a little while. Then Ed and Jax had to leave to meet up with Mom and Dad to talk to the Ebrinites about the plans to close up all the portals or rift openings on the map. Ed wanted to be sure that only the portal near the Market of Caltrez would be left open. They couldn't take the chance that R. L. would use one of the six portals to escape or steal everything from another city. Ed was working to cover all the bases this time. This defensive move would help them keep R. L. where they wanted him. They couldn't afford to let him slip away from them again.

The one open portal would allow Ed and Mel to go back to their world with Jax and find the baby dragons. Ed asked the Ebrinite engineers about the plan details.

Student text:

"So, even if the small shell from the small box opens up a rift, these sheds will keep anybody from getting past?" Ed said.

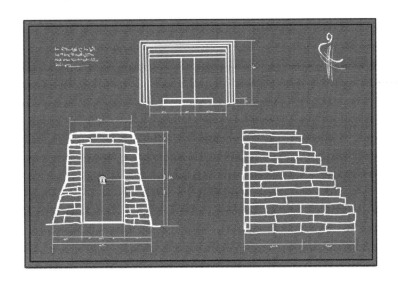

"Yes, we will put the small sheds on the exits. We will apply rock, cement, and metal access panels with strong locks to the sheds. Each shed will have a lookout to <u>watch</u> it all hours of the day. R. L. will not get back into Ebrin through these rift openings," the Ebrin man said.

Ed was happy with the progress. He said to Jax, "These skillful people are doing this job well. The investment in this project will help us significantly."

"Now, what equipment do you think we need for the trip to get the stuff for Mel to craft the meds?" Ed did ask.

"Ed, do you think we can do this? You know, get the Shadow Jellyfish?" Jax did ask.

"I don't know Jax. But we have to try. I know this spell Mel and I have to combat is one that can't be . . . um, see, I can't find how to fully say what I want now. The spell is there to stop us. That's it. I am sick of it, but what do we do? It can depress you, but the dragon did remind me that the bad stuff is not the only thing to think about.

"Mel and I did find Mom and Dad when we should not have. That was a win. We just have to do the one next step and go from there. If we stop now, then we have lost."

Jax said, "It isn't painless, is it?"

"No," said Ed. "But it is <u>worth</u> it. All of this is going to pay off."

"Okay," said Jax. "Let's look at what we need to get a Shadow Jellyfish."

Game to play: Lock It Up

Help the Ebrinite engineers lock up the portal gates.

Materials needed:
- Game board and game cards. See Game Appendix.
- Optional: game tokens or counting chips to use instead of lock cards.

Rules:
1. Shuffle the word cards and put them in a pile face down.
2. Player One draws a card and reads it. They will find the suffix used at the end of the word on the map (game board). There is a suffix for each gate. The player will place a Player One lock card in the box.
3. It is now Player Two's turn.
4. If a card can't be played, the player puts it in the discard pile and their turn is over.
5. The first player to lock all the portal gates by placing one of their lock cards at each gate wins.

Chapter 3

Narrator (Parent or Tutor):

Meanwhile, R. L. Nox was making his own preparations. "Fred! I need an update on the circus. Tell me about the dragon pens and the advertisement fliers! What is going on with the dragons? Is that girl from Ebrin doing what we are telling her?" R. L. Nox belted out. "Now, Fred! Don't waste my time."

Fred rushed over to R. L.'s office. It had been very busy around the warehouse and the circus down the road. Fred had made all the arrangements to purchase the small circus. The owner wasn't too fond of the idea of selling it, but R. L. made him an offer he couldn't ignore. R. L. also made the idea of not selling the circus less appealing. The owner figured he would rather get rich by selling the circus than finding himself stuck all alone in another world where he would be eaten by horrible dragons. He saw R. L.'s dragon babies and trusted everything R. L. said about their parents.

Now that R. L. owned a circus, Fred had a lot of new responsibilities. He managed all the new employees that came with the circus. He delegated work such as ordering supplies for all the circus animals and printing fliers for the new attraction. One job he wouldn't delegate was calling the world-famous Tashkent Circus back. Getting a spot to perform in their circus wasn't an easy thing to do, but he was confident they would come to an arrangement. Dragons and the Tashkent Circus would be an amazing combination.

Fred still had all his old responsibilities to take care of as well. He was still responsible for managing the storefront and the online store. Some inventory needed to be moved over to his coworker running the black-market sales. Selling those items at the regular store would bring unwanted attention from the police.

Fred's favorite part of the job, though, was taking care of the dragons with Bree. He was amazed by the dragons. He loved that they were real and not just mythical creatures. The dragons' eyes were fierce yet had a gentleness in them. The dragons connected with Fred in a way that made him feel like he was valuable. That was different from how R. L. would make him feel. "Fred, what's your problem? Fred, you are too slow. Fred, why do I put up with you?"

Fred was also thankful for Bree. R. L. had kidnapped Bree when he stole the dragons. Fred felt a little guilty keeping Bree here. She wasn't happy about it, but she cared for the dragons more than her freedom. She made sure the dragons had everything they needed. That made his job easier. And Bree was kind to Fred even though he was not allowing her to leave. She was even kind in how she made it known that she wasn't happy there and that it was wrong to keep the dragons and her away from Ebrin.

"FRED!" R. L. screamed again. R. L. could be so impatient. It was like he thought the world existed just to please him. Fred stepped into R. L.'s office.

Student text:

"Yes, boss," Fred said.

"So . . . tell me the news," R. L. said.

"Things are going well. They are finishing up the final details on dragon pens now. They are setting up the feeding bins and the sky walk trail above the pens. The shredded hay did ship out on Friday. I expect it this evening. The dragons can be put in the pens by the end of the week.

"Also, the crew is planning the dragon show and is making significant progress. They are getting excited to have an amazing main show.

"Bree has been doing what she is told to

do. She has been training the dragons to get in and out of the small pens. You could say they are kennel training. The dragons follow her commands well. I have to say, she is amazing."

R. L. shot Fred an aggravated look.

Fred did continue, "The dragons are playing with the balls and pumpkins we have been giving them. I think people will pay to see them play.

"All is well there except that the dragons are beginning to sleep an extra hour, maybe two. Bree doesn't know why."

"Keep an eye on it," R. L. said. "What about the other things?"

"Well, the print shop omitted the hours on the ad. They will print them again and mail them by the end of the day.

"The shops are getting a lot of traffic and making a lot of cash. So all is going well there. I think there is too much cash for us to go to the bank. I decided to get a bank truck. It will pick up our deposit at the end of the day."

"That is all, Fred." R. L. yelled. He jotted a few things on his tablet as Fred left R. L.'s tent.

Fred was passing by the dragon pen when Bree began to hug a dragon. The other one began to push her with its wing. It was begging for a hug. Fred rested against a tree to <u>watch</u> the dragons for a bit. Bree extended her hand to the second dragon. It folded its wing and trotted to her to get his hug. It let out what must have been a dragon laugh. Bree had a big grin.

Fred left to finish his job for the day. He had a big grin too.

Game to play: Dragon Hugs

Some days can be rough with too much work to do and grumpy people to deal with. Hugs can make those days a little better. Look for the Dragon Hug spots to help your game.

Materials needed:
- Game board and game cards. See Game Appendix.
- A game token for each player.
- Six-sided die.

Rules:
1. Player One draws a card and reads it.
2. Player One rolls the die and moves their game token that number of spaces.
3. Follow any directions on the game board space.
4. It is now Player Two's turn.
5. The first player who reaches "The End" wins the game.

Chapter 4

Additional required skills for student text:

Ability to read words with the various sounds of suffix -ed.

Barton Level: **Level 5 Lesson 4**.

Narrator (Parent or Tutor):

Ed's plan was in motion. The engineers and builders reported back that work was going well on the sturdy sheds guarding the doorways to Ed and Mel's world. Only the doorway near the Caltrez market would remain open.

Boxes full of tents and supplies lay in groups on the ground. They were being loaded up for the return trip to Caltrez. Only flattened grass remained where the camp once stood.

The merchants were ready to go back to their homes near the Caltrez market. They were eager to see how the rebuilding efforts were going in the market. They heard how people in the surrounding towns were coming to help the recovery efforts. Craftsmen and craftswomen were busy at work making new things to sell. They wanted to get their shops rebuilt and get back to work. It had been awhile since things had been normal.

The disruption had been worth it, though. If Ed hadn't led them into battle, R. L. would have killed the dragons to steal their gold. Even though R. L. ransacked the market while they were gone, they had saved the Felkin. The dragons had healed from their wounds and were safe.

In the middle of all the packing, the Felkin bellowed their goodbyes. They shot a few flames into the air to express their thanks before entering the mine opening in the side of the hill. They were going back to mine gold and tend the gas vents deep in the ground underneath the grassy plains. One Felkin stayed top side with the Ebrinites to help fly some supplies back to Caltrez.

Mom and Dad were heading to Caltrez as well. They wanted to see Ed, Mel, and Jax off through the doorway to their world before taking supplies to the town of Jalisp. Gathering and delivering the supplies would help take their minds off of the dangers Ed and Mel faced. Jalisp needed the supplies, as construction was to start on the meeting hall that R. L. burned down. Mom and Dad would gather windows and lighting fixtures while Ed, Mel, and Jax gathered the ingredients for the dragon's medicine. After they delivered the supplies, they would wait with their friends in Caltrez to hear from Ed, Mel, and Jax.

Ed, Mel, and Jax were ready to leave. The last thing Mel had to do was to leave Ash with her parents. There was no way that she could take him on the journey to Endless Bay. He couldn't go with her to her world either. He would bring too much unwanted attention. An animal like Ash would definitely stand out as unusual and exotic in her world. His energy and cuteness made everyone notice him and want to watch him. Well, almost everyone. Mel remembered when Ed ran away and left her when he first saw Ash. Anyway, the extra attention he would bring would hamper their efforts to catch R. L. If they were going to catch him, they needed to be able to surprise him. She gave the furry little guy a big hug and kiss good-bye.

Student text:

"Mom and Dad, thanks for <u>watch</u>ing Ash for me," said Mel. "We love you both so much!"

"We love you too," Mom answered. "You <u>watch</u> out, you three."

"We will." Mel spun back to Ed and Jax. "Are you both all set to go?" Mel asked.

"Yep," Ed answered. "Let's get these items and go rescue the baby dragons!"

Jax added, "The big Felkin is going to fly us to the Laughfully Tree stand next to Endless Bay. We can walk to Endless Bay from there."

"It will meet us at Endless Bay in 24-

hours to fly us back to Caltrez," Jax finished.

"Ed, fancy that," Mel laughed. "We get to travel by dragon!"

Ed gulped, "Yep, fancy that." Ed was just glad that the Felkin was helping them cut six days of travel off of their trip. He was thankful for their help even if the thought of riding on a dragon's back was a bit intimidating.

The trip itself wasn't as intimidating as Ed thought it was going to be. In fact, it was thrilling to be above the fog and mist in the sky. The dragon was very confident in his flying skills. Ed couldn't wait for the trip back.

The dragon landed next to the stand of Laughfully Trees. Ed, Mel, and Jax quickly hopped off into the deep grass. Mel thanked the dragon. Then he flew back up into the sky.

"Who wants to go up the tree to milk the rats?" Mel asked.

"Are you crazy?" Ed exclaimed. "I can't stand rats and these rats look extra big."

"I didn't want to go if you wanted to do it," Mel kidded. "Jax, how about you?"

"If you don't mind, I'll let you do it Mel," Jax responded. "Can you get up the tree okay?"

"You bet I can," Mel said.

Mel went up the tree and followed what Doc had told her in his lessons. The rats were friendly. It happened to be that Mel was excellent at milking tree rats. She was done in an hour.

"See, this is why she is going to be an excellent vet," Ed explained to Jax. Jax grinned and nodded.

As Mel finished milking the tree rats, Ed and Jax had picked the plants that they needed. The Ebrin Lily and the Indigo Bunch Grass plants grew below the Laughfully Trees in big patches.

Mel put the jug of rat milk into her backpack. Ed and Jax handed her the plants to put in her pack.

"Well, the stress-free jobs are completed," Jax said. "Shall we walk to Endless Bay now?"

"Yes," Ed responded. "Let's do this."

Mel nodded and held Jax's hand as they walked on the path to Endless Bay.

Game to play: Sounds of the Past

Three ingredients gathered. Three sounds of -ed. The number three seemed to be coming up a lot, recently, Mel thought. Play a game of threes. Use the three sounds of -ed to move through the game board of triangles.

Materials needed:
- Game board and game cards. See Game Appendix.
- A game token for each player.

Rules:
1. Place the game tokens on the "Start" space.
2. Player One draws a card and reads it.
    a. If the word ends in the sound /t/, the player finds the "t" on the triangle where their token is. They will move to the triangle next to the "t" or follow the arrow next to the "t."
    b. If the word ends in the sound /d/, the player finds the "d" on the triangle where their token is. They will move to the triangle next to the "d" or follow the arrow next to the "d."
    c. If the word ends in the sounds /ed/, the player finds the "ed" on the triangle where their token is. They will move to the triangle next to the "ed" or follow the arrow next to the "ed."
3. It is now Player Two's turn.
4. Reshuffle the cards as needed.
5. The first player to move into a triangle with the word "END" wins the game.

Chapter 5

Narrator (Parent or Tutor):

It only took the trio a few hours to walk to Endless Bay. There was one small village next to the bay. The Ebrinites who lived there gave Ed, Mel, and Jax a warm welcome and invited them to dinner.

Over dinner, the Ebrinites learned the reason for Ed, Mel, and Jax's visit to the village. Like Jax, they were astonished and overwhelmed with the idea of catching a Shadow Jellyfish. Even the old, experienced fishermen were doubtful it could be done. Yes, the villagers told stories to their children of how their ancestors had captured a Shadow Jellyfish to save a few dragons of long ago who wandered back to the old land for a visit, but they never had seen anyone actually do it.

Yet, there didn't seem to be much of a choice. They understood the importance of the dragons in their ecosystem. The people needed the dragons to quiet the tremors in the ground. When R. L. took the baby dragons, this cycle was broken. It was only a matter of time before Ebrin would be uninhabitable. They also understood the dragons needed the jellyfish in order to be cured of the toxin. The Ebrinite children wouldn't have a future in Ebrin if they did nothing.

Because of this, the Ebrin villagers were eager to help, but they were too afraid to actually capture a Shadow Jellyfish themselves. Ed, Mel, and Jax were going to have to do that part alone.

They started out early in the morning as the sun rose. The sun looked like it was coming out from the water of the bay. The old Ebrinite fisherman sailed his boat directly towards the rising sun. Ed, Mel, and Jax were getting ready to swim in the deep water. They were putting on gear that would allow them to breathe underwater. It was very similar to scuba gear that Ed and Mel had used before, but they weren't going to have to worry about a big tank or running out of air. This gear had a special filter that pulled the air out of the water for them to breathe.

The boat changed directions. They were getting close. Mel checked the container and the long poles that would help them direct the Shadow Jellyfish into the container. The night before they had spent more than an hour running through the plan on land. In a few minutes they would find out if it was going to work.

Student text:

"How are you doing, Ed?" Mel asked.

"Let's just say I'll be happy when this is done," Ed said timidly.

"I agree," said Jax. He was getting restless. "This is the wildest and stupidest thing I've done. If we upset the Shadow Jellyfish, you will know. They will begin to glow, and we will be enveloped in a mass of angry animals. They will all attack and we will be done for."

The old fisherman piped up, "This is outlandish. I know it has to be done, but let me know if you want me to go back. I won't think badly of you all."

"No," Mel said confidently. "I'll do this."

The old fisherman said, "You are the bravest gal I know, Mel, but you are still a bit clueless to the risk. Well, this is it."

Mel sat and dipped her leg into the bay. It was chilly but not too cold. She slid into the bay. Jax and Ed handed her the expandable container. Jax slipped into the bay. Ed handed him the long sticks. Then

Ed slid into the bay too. He didn't want to splash.

They could see the smack of jellyfish about fifteen feet away. Mel shot Ed and Jax a gritty, strong-minded look and nodded. Then she slowly sank into the deep. Ed and Jax followed.

It was difficult to see the Shadow Jellyfish in the shimmery liquid of the bay. Shadow was a spot-on way to tell someone about the jellyfish. Shadows stacked upon shadows. Mel had difficulty telling what was a true shadow from the jellyfish and the sun and what was a jellyfish.

She stayed calm. She drew upon her

animal training know-how and <u>watch</u>ed. She didn't know how predictable the jellyfish were, but she was going to <u>watch</u> them to find out how they swam. The complexity of their swimming was stunning. Mel could <u>watch</u> them for hours.

Mel tossed out a small rock to <u>watch</u> how the jellyfish acted with it. They didn't do much at all. Then she sent a small fish to swim into the jellyfish. Almost instantly, the fish was covered by jellyfish and stung. It was still and began to float, not swim.

Before long, Mel picked up on the tempo of the jellyfish. She picked out a jellyfish and slowly began to lift her long stick. If she could coax it away from the others, this difficult task was attainable.

The jellyfish paid no thought to the stick which was slowly pulling it away from the others. Jax and Ed helped keep it from floating back to the smack with their long sticks. Slowly, slowly it approached Mel's container.

And then, Mel trapped it! Mel was a jellyfish trapper. She began to swim up to the boat when Jax swam up to her and stuck his hand in front of her floating hair.

The next moment, Jax went limp and still. Behind Jax's hand a shadow began to glow. Mel had almost swum into a Shadow

Jellyfish. She hadn't seen it. Jax did, and he blocked its sting with his hand.

Mel began to panic. Ed grabbed her hand and Jax. He pulled up. Mel held on to the container. The jellyfish in it began to glow. She grabbed Jax with her other hand. Ed and Mel quickly swam up to the boat. The glow of jellyfish grew behind them.

The old fisherman helped pull Jax onto the boat. He was sad but not shocked. "Get in the boat quickly!" he said.

Ed and Mel didn't delay. They got into the boat just before the angry, glowing jellyfish got a hold of Mel's heel.

The fisherman handed Ed a canteen. "Put this on the sting, but don't contact the sting with your hands. We need to get to land now! Is the jellyfish contained?" he asked.

Mel looked at the jellyfish glowing in the container and said, "Yes, it is. Will Jax be okay?"

"Um, well, uh . . . probably not," the old fisherman responded. "But we won't quit on him yet! There may be a small possibility that he'll pull out of it if we get him to land."

"Well then, step on it!" Mel yelled.

Game to play: Jellyfish Capture

Capturing a jellyfish isn't the easiest task. See if you can catch the Shadow Jellyfish.

Materials needed:
- Game cards. See Game Appendix.

Rules:
1. Shuffle the cards and place them all face down in a grid.
2. Player One will turn two cards over.
    a. If the words on the cards use the same suffix, it is a match. If a match is made, Player One will pick up the cards and then take another turn.
    b. If a match is not made, the player will turn the cards back over. It is now Player Two's turn.
3. If the jellyfish picture card is turned over, the container picture card must also be turned over to catch the jellyfish.
    a. If both pictures are turned over for a match, the player picks up the cards, and the game will continue until all the cards are matched. The player will count the jellyfish-container match as two matches when counting up their score.
    b. If the jellyfish card is turned over and not matched with the container picture card, the player automatically loses the game.

Chapter 6

Additional required skills for student text:

Ability to read words when y changes to i with an added suffix.

Barton Level: **Level 5 Lesson 6**.

Note: The words "school" and "chemistry" are used out of order from the Barton scope and sequence.

Narrator (Parent or Tutor):

The old fisherman concentrated on turning the boat around for a speedy return to shore. Ed slowly poured the contents of the canteen over Jax's sting. It had a strong, bitter smell and bubbled along the wound.

Mel glanced back and forth from the jellyfish in the container to Jax. How could something so beautiful, graceful, and small cause the horrible anxiety, pressure, and tremendous guilt she felt? It was almost she who was laying there unconscious. It should have been her. But now, her best friend was dying. Was Jax really her best friend? Mel realized that he was indeed her best friend.

The village had prepared for the likely worst-case scenario. When they saw the boat speeding to shore, they knew what had happened. The skill of the old fisherman, the tide, and the direction of the wind all helped the boat reach the shore in record time. The villagers worked quickly to get Jax off the boat and into their doctor's care. His chance for survival was small, but they would do everything they could to increase that chance. It was their part to help save the baby dragons and Ebrin.

The old fisherman turned to Ed and Mel. "I am so sorry about your friend. I hate to do this, but I must remind you of your task. Your journey is important. It is why you risked your lives. You will not be able to stop to wait and see how Jax is doing. You must continue.

"My friend will help you clip the five Shadow Jellyfish tentacles that you need for the medicine. Then you must leave. The Felkin is already here to take you back to Caltrez. We will return the jellyfish to the sea. These jellyfish regrow their tentacles, so it will be fine.

"We will take good care of Jax and will send any news of Jax, good or bad, right away."

The next few hours flew by in a haze. With the Shadow Jellyfish tentacles safely next to the Tree Rat milk, the Ebrin lily, and the Indigo Bunch Grass in Mel's backpack, the Felkin took Ed and Mel back to Caltrez. They explained everything that had happened as they prepared to go through the portal back to their world. Did they have all the ingredients for the dragon's medicine? Did they have the map from R. L.'s house that showed where the portal opened up in their world? Did they still have some cash from their world?

Soon, they were ready to return to their world.

Student text:

"I don't want to go," Mel said. "I feel that I am abandoning Jax and Ebrin. I think I am a bit timid about meeting R. L. too."

"Mel, Jax would want you to continue. He won't quit. He was bold with that jellyfish. You need to keep being bold too," Dad replied.

"I've tried. I don't feel bold now. I have a pit in my gut, and I don't think I could feel any yuckier," Mel answered.

"If I always went by how I felt, I wouldn't have done a lot of things, Mel," Dad said. "This is difficult. So, just one step is needed now. Okay? Then you can try the next step. You two are the gutsiest and bravest kids I know. I don't envy your task, but I know you are reliable and can do this."

Ed added, "With all the mess and distress R. L. has put us through, I am not afraid for you, Mel, when we meet R. L. He is the one who should be afraid when he sees you. Remember how you let that nasty kid have it when he put that cat in a bag to toss it away? Let's finish this hunt."

With that, Ed and Mel hugged Mom and Dad and stepped into the rift. They followed the dim tunnel all the way to the door that opened to their land. The map said that Tashkent, Uzbekistan was just beyond the door. "So, this is the next step," Mel said as she opened the door.

Ed spied past the door. He saw train tracks below. Just beyond that were some empty benches. "It looks okay," he said.

Ed and Mel dashed out from the hidden door, ran past the train tracks, and sat on one of the benches. No one spotted them exiting the door. They sat for a bit, and then Mel asked, "Ed, do you recall that <u>school</u> we visited with our parents a few years back? It was in Tashkent, wasn't it?"

"Yes, I think it was," Ed replied.

"That <u>school</u> has a crazy <u>chemistry</u> lab. It will have all the things I need to craft the meds. Shall we go see if it is still there?" Mel asked.

"Yep. I think that would be a grand next step," Ed grinned.

Game to play: Changes

As Ed and Mel traveled through the portal, they reflected on the differences between their world and Ebrin. The color of the sky was different, for instance. But even though there were differences between the worlds, they were still connected. There is still a connection to the base word when a suffix changes the spelling of y to i. Read words with these changes to travel through the portal door to Tashkent.

Materials needed:
- Game board and game cards. See Game Appendix.
- A game token for each player.

Rules:
1. Place the game cards in a pile face down.
2. Player One will draw a card and read all the words on the card.
3. Player One will count the words on the card and move that number of spaces on the gameboard. If there is one word on the card, Player One will move one space. If there are three words on the card, Player One will move three spaces.
4. It is now Player Two's turn.
5. The first person to reach "The End" wins the game.

Chapter 7

Narrator (Parent or Tutor):

Ed and Mel exited the train station. The blue sky above reminded them that they were definitely back in their world. It was good to see the familiar sky, but somehow it didn't feel like they were returning home. They had grown fond of the pale green Ebrin sky. The different colored sky reminded them of what they were fighting for, and they quickly found their way to the international school in Tashkent. School had just finished, and there were students and teachers bustling down the halls. Ed and Mel made their way to the chemistry lab. Mel had remembered correctly. The chemistry lab had all sorts of equipment. It was well funded to provide a top-notch science education for the school's students.

They were in luck. The chemistry teacher was still in the lab.

"Hello, I'm Mel, and this is Ed," Mel introduced herself and her brother. The teacher looked up. Mel said, "Hello. We need your help. Can we rent your lab? We don't have much cash, but it is important that I have access to a lab."

The teacher looked Ed and Mel up and down. "Sorry. This lab is for the school's students only. If you have something important, take it elsewhere," the teacher briskly said.

"We don't have much, well, we have to get this done quickly. I know it may . . . well, there is a . . ." Mel almost said "a dragon." Instead she said, "There is an animal that needs a med that I have to craft or it will . . . it will . . . croak, you know, as in pass away. I need a chem lab to craft the med," Mel responded.

"You don't have much what? Time? Then take your animal to a vet. I don't get why you want to use my chemistry lab. This isn't a lab to craft medicines and potions like you would in a video game. I told you this lab is only for students of this school. Even if you were students of this school, you would have to prove you have the skills to use this lab. Besides, I would recommend that you work on your English lessons before doing extra-curricular activities in chemistry. You can't even communicate a clear and complete thought. I doubt you would have the skills to work in this lab. You may leave now," the teacher directed.

Mel opened her mouth to plead more with the teacher when he stood up and directed them to the door. Ed and Mel turned around and went into the hall. The teacher's words stung. The spell was difficult enough, but the attitude of the teacher added another layer of difficulty. If she could only explain. But then again, why would the teacher believe that dragons were real.

Just across the hallway, a boy was staring at Ed and Mel. After the teacher closed the door behind Ed and Mel, he came over to them and locked eyes with Mel.

Student text:

Finally, the student began to talk. "Mr. Stump can be nasty. He has a reputation for not having compassion if you don't study in the way he thinks is best. I'm Lucas, and I'm <u>dyslexic</u>. Mr. Stump thinks my accommodations show that I am lazy. 'If you would just try, you wouldn't need accommodations,' he tells me. I don't think he'll help you.

"What do you need with the chem lab anyway? And you best tell me the <u>truth</u> because I can tell when someone isn't telling me the <u>truth</u>," Lucas said.

"Well, I am glad that you mentioned that. That talent will be helpful because the <u>truth</u> is a tiny bit crazy," said Mel. Ed shot Mel a funny look.

Mel added, "Okay, it is a lot of crazy with a crazy problem and a crazy solution. The chem lab . . . um, it is a fraction of the solution."

"Go on," Lucas replied.

Mel continued, "The most relevant info is that I need the chem lab to craft a med to put into a shot. The injection is the one thing that will rescue some baby dragons from a toxin that is . . . um, that is in this spot . . . er, this land.

"You see, the dragons were stolen from Ebrin and are now somewhere in Tashkent, that is if they haven't left yet. The toxin is new to them.

"Ed and I risked being killed to get the components for the meds. Our friend may still .

. . he may still pass away because he helped us." Mel held back from crying. She looked back at Lucas. She had Lucas's full attention.

Lucas asked, "Ok. I can tell you are telling the truth, but did you say dragons? And, what is 'Ebrin'?"

"Yes, she did," Ed said.

Ed and Mel explained to Lucas what was going on. Mel showed him the components for the meds. They told him about Ebrin and about R. L. Nox.

Lucas was convinced that they were telling the truth. He decided to help them, and they developed a plan.

That evening Ed and Mel were scanning Lucas's lab pass at the chem lab door. The dim glow from their lamps helped Mel see the equipment but not the rat hiding in the shadows. She just had to listen to the scratching on the floor to know it was there. But as rodents do, it quickly hid from Ed and Mel.

Mel pulled out the app Lucas had lent her. It had OCR and text-to-speech. With it she could quickly find all the equipment and supplies she needed. It also helped her with the equipment

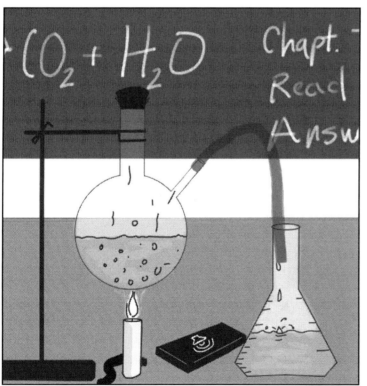

directions.

Before long, Mel was finished crafting the meds. As they began to chill in a flask, she began to wash up.

She didn't want Lucas getting a detention if she left a mess behind in the lab.

Suddenly, there was a thud behind her. Mel twisted back to look at the flask. The rat had walked across the top of the flask. Its prints were evident on the flask. It had fallen. That was the thud. Now the rat just sat there. Mel picked it up.

"What are you doing, Mel?" Ed asked. "Rats have illnesses."

"Ed, look at this rat," Mel said. "It isn't afraid. It is acting odd for a rat. It is as if its mind is blank or that it can't recall how to be a rat. Look, that look in its eye says 'confusion.'"

"No way!" Ed exclaimed. "I bet that is why Doc told you to not get any of the potion on you. It is a med for the dragons but toxic for us. And for rats, it seems. Let's get the potion into the shots for the dragons and scram. The sun is beginning to come up. We can hand the rat to Lucas to keep for now."

Game to play: SION/TION Reaction

Mel couldn't read all the chemical names and equipment directions, but she wasn't going to let that stop her. She used text-to-speech to get her work done. She also knew that all her studying was helping her regain those skills. In fact, while she and Ed were waiting for the right time to enter the lab, they studied -tion and -sion. Ed, of course, made their flashcards into a game.

Materials needed:
- Game board and game cards. See Game Appendix.
- Optional: game tokens or counting chips.

Rules:
1. Player One draws a card, reads the word, and places the card or a token on the game board in the appropriate hexagon.
   a. Use the tion /shun/ hexagon for words ending in "tion" – A total of three cards are to be placed in this hexagon noted by the "triple bond" notation.
   b. Use the sion /zhun/ hexagon for words ending in "sion" with the /zhun/ pronunciation – A total of two cards are to be placed in this hexagon noted by the "double bond" notation.
   c. Use the sion /shun/ hexagon for words ending in sion with the /shun/ pronunciation – One card is to be placed in this hexagon noted by the "single bond" notation.
   d. If the hexagon is full, place the card in the discard file.
2. It is now Player Two's turn.
3. The first player to fill their chemical compound on the game board with a total of six cards or tokens wins the game.

Chapter 8

Additional required skills for student text:

Ability to read words with the prefixes: dis-, in-, un-, and non-.

Barton Level: **Level 5 Lesson 8**.

Note: The word "circus" is used out of order from the Barton scope and sequence. USD = U. S. Dollars.

Narrator (Parent or Tutor):

R. L. sat in his air-conditioned office with his feet up on his desk, his eyes closed, and his hands behind his head. He thought of his increasing wealth. He thought of the dragons and the fame they would bring him. He thought of how others would respect him and want to be like him. Maybe the success and attention would stop the voices from his past, which still haunted him.

"R. L. you'll never amount to anything."

"R. L. how stupid can you be?"

"R. L. Nox is dumb as a box of rocks!"

"Why do I waste my time with you? Will you ever learn?"

He didn't feel guilty that he was hurting others in his plans to get rich. People had hurt him, so what did it matter if he passed some of the hurt on. If people were too weak to deal with it, that was their problem. He deserved the empire he was building.

Fred knocked on R. L.'s door. "I've got the daily report ready, boss."

"Tell me what I want to hear, Fred," R. L. said.

"Well, the fliers have been delivered all around town. I've mailed more to neighboring cities. I have the video production team scheduled to make the video for the world-wide commercials.

"For the supply report, all the supplies and branded merchandise have been delivered. Regular deliveries have been set up. The dragon enclosure is ready for business.

"I've posted extra security. All the staff we need have been hired. Almost everything is ready for opening day," Fred finished.

"Almost. What do you mean 'almost' you moron?" R. L. snipped.

Fred shifted his weight from one foot to the other. This was the news that he was dreading giving to R. L.

"Well . . . it's the dragons. They aren't looking too good. Bree says they are sick," Fred said.

R. L.'s eyes narrowed with a building rage.

Fred continued, "I have an excellent large animal vet coming in fifteen minutes. I'm sure we will get them healthy by opening day."

"How could you let this happen? Do you know what this means to me? You better fix this or you will be sorry!" R. L. sneered. "Go! Get out of here! Fix this now!"

"Yes, boss! Right away, boss!" Fred said as he rushed out of the office. He didn't want to be in there a second longer than he had to be.

Fred met Bree at the dragon's pen. She was crying. He gave her a hug and looked down into her face.

"Fred, I don't know what is happening to the dragons. The small one is now refusing to eat. I'm so worried about them," Bree said.

"Hush now, Bree. I have the vet coming. She is the best vet in Uzbekistan. I don't care if R. L. just wants fame and money. I want the dragons to get well and be safe, just like you do," Fred said.

"Why don't you send them back to Ebrin then?" Bree asked.

"You know I can't do that. Helping the dragons get better is one thing. Crossing R. L. by letting them go is another. R. L. would have my skin. Besides,

I owe him. He saved me from the slums. I had no job, no family, nothing. If it wasn't for R. L. I'd probably be dead," Fred finished.

"He just uses you," Bree replied. "I know the difference between caring for someone and using them. He may have helped you, but you don't owe him a thing."

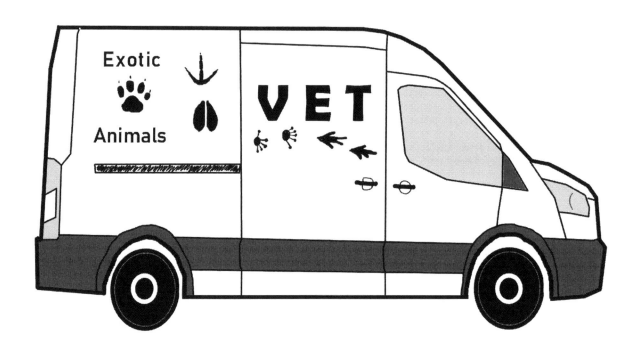

Student text:

At that exact moment, Ed and Mel were picking up a <u>circus</u> flier at a shop across the city. Mel and Ed felt drained, as they didn't get much sleep, but they unselfishly drifted through the city looking for hints about where the dragons could be.

They had been unsuccessful in finding any hint about the dragons' location. That is, until they picked up the flier.

"Ed, do you see this? It tells us exactly where the baby dragons are!" Mel exclaimed. "Ooh, this is uncalled for. R. L. is putting the dragons in a <u>circus</u>. That is so unfair to Ebrin and the dragons. Look at this. A yearly pass to the <u>circus</u> with unlimited visits is 'only $10,000 USD a person.' That is indecent to ask that much."

"Mel, look at the T.V. in that shop," Ed said. "There is an ad for the <u>circus</u> on the screen. There are a lot of people paying attention to it.

"There will be people there nonstop once the <u>circus</u> opens. Look at the hours. The main hours are 6:00 AM to 10:00 PM and then evening shifts are available to <u>watch</u> the dragons sleep. If we don't get to them before it opens, we may be unable to rescue the dragons."

"I'm not going to wait any longer," Mel responded. "Look, we can catch a bus to go that way in 90 seconds. Let's go across the street to the bus stop."

Before long Ed and Mel stepped off of the bus in front of the <u>circus</u>. Its tents were grand. Big flags with dragons flew by the doorway. Smaller ones flew along the paths between the <u>circus</u> tents. A van with a vet logo was in front of the main door. Mel looked at Ed.

"Do you think we are unlucky and we delayed too long?" Mel asked.

"There is only one way to find out," said Ed.

They ran past the van to the doorway. A watchman stopped them.

"No entry kids. You will have to wait until opening day. Now get lost," the watchman said.

Ed and Mel left the main entry door, but they snuck back to the back lot. When the circus people were distracted, Ed unscrewed a chain link panel. He held it up for Mel to creep past. He followed and put the panel back into its spot.

From their hiding spot, Mel could see the dragons, the vet, Fred, and Bree. "Ed, look! There they are! Bree is there too!"

Bree was sitting next to a baby dragon

facing Mel. Fred's back was to Ed and Mel. The vet was disinfecting her hands.

Mel had a lot less stress now that she could see the dragons, but she could see they needed the meds badly. The lethal effect of the toxin was now inevitable without the meds.

She was about to tell Ed that she thought she could distract Bree and get her attention when she felt a strong hand grab the back of her neck.

Mel and Ed had been apprehended.

Game to play: Game of Not

Sometimes it is easier to describe something by saying what it is not. Ed and Mel are unhappy and unlucky to have been caught. During the untimely encounter, all Mel could think was, "Not now!"

Materials needed:
- Game board and game cards. See Game Appendix.
- Two game tokens.
- Six-sided die.

Rules:
1. Player One draws a card and reads it.
2. Player One rolls the die and moves their game token that number of spaces.
3. It is now Player Two's turn.
4. Follow the directions on the game board. When a player reaches the end of the "N" they will continue on to the "O." Game play will continue from the "O" to the "T" to "The End." The first player who reaches "The End" wins the game.

Chapter 9

Additional required skills for student text:

Ability to read words with the prefixes mis-, sub-, re-, and pre-.

Sight Words: talk, chalk, always, own, build, buy, awful, else, truth, often, honest, pretty, tough, mountain.

Barton Level: **Level 5 Lesson 9**.

Narrator (Parent or Tutor):

When Ed and Mel had been caught, they put up a fight and created quite a commotion. Bree noticed them and started to run to them, but one of the security guards stopped her. Bree started to fight him and was winning until three other guards came. In the background the baby dragons were bellowing, radios were chattering, and they could hear R. L. starting to yell commands in the distance. Ed, Mel, and Bree couldn't fight off all the guards.

Now, Ed and Mel sat in silence in an old lion cage in one of the small tents. It was dark in the tent, and the cage still smelled like the big cat that once slept there. Mel would have felt better if only they had been able to talk to Bree and give her the medicine for the baby dragons. Mel held her backpack with the medicine close. At least they hadn't taken her bag away. The medicine was still safe.

Mel pleaded with the guard watching them. She asked to just talk to Bree or even the vet, but he completely ignored her. It was of no use.

The tent door opened and sunlight streamed through. At first Ed and Mel shielded their eyes from the sudden brightness, but it was quickly dimmed by the figure stepping into the tent. R. L. Nox looked down at the cage. A grin spread across his face, and he started to laugh.

Student text:

"Well, well, look at you two. This has developed into an awful situation, hasn't it?" R. L. said.

Mel yelled, "Let the dragons go! They don't belong to you!"

R. L.'s grin dissolved. "I think we need to have a conversation," R. L. replied as he pulled up a chair.

"You know, I regret having to put a spell on you two, but I discovered that I have to do what I have to do to get what I want. I don't expect anyone to help me. In fact, people are often against me.

"You see, I had difficulty with words

when I was a child. No one helped me if I misspelled a word. They put me in the back of the class. They said I had a preexisting condition and that I was subhuman because I couldn't succeed at their stupid tests. Year after year I listened to them.

"Then one day I punched Billy Smith in the gut for calling me a misfit. I was going to hit him again, but I picked up his lunch and left with it. It was a yummy lunch.

"The next day, Billy handed me another lunch. That

tiny mishap let me reclaim my dignity. I have come across bigger lunches to grab, if you know what I am saying.

"Now, with Ebrin I think there are some readjustments that need to happen. Ebrin has hidden away its riches for many years. Why have they hidden them? Think about it. Our people could benefit too. Ebrin has hidden their riches for long enough."

"You want to benefit from their riches. You don't think of other people," Ed cut in.

R. L. replied, "I bet it looks that way. The tactics I've had to apply to the situation misrepresent my intentions."

"I think your actions show your

intentions well enough," Ed said.

"Ah, yes. Well . . . that brings me to my request," R. L continued. "You know this wasn't planned to be such a big production with my hasty collection of supplies, this misdirected hunt of yours, and all.

"I just needed your parents to help me for a bit. The spell was to help you wait at your hut for us. You would have been reunited again. You should have just waited for them, and then the spell would have been lifted. The dragons would still be in Ebrin, too. I didn't plan on taking them.

"So, I am asking that you just stop this madness. Let me be. Your actions led us to where we are now. Accept responsibility. Accept the results of your actions, and stop instigating problems.

"I know it may be difficult for you to stop your hunt, so I present this option to you.

"Look the other way. Let me be, and I will get rid of this ugly spell. You will always have to try to function with it if I don't help you. I am the only one who can help you with this.

"Ebrin won't remember what it cost you to help them. They will be hidden away again after this. Anyway, how could they respect you for all the unrest in their land because of you. There wasn't any conflict in Ebrin before you showed up, so it wasn't me who began this mess," R. L. finished.

"Think about it," he said as he walked out of the tent.

Mel wanted to yell at R. L. but the notion of having the spell lifted was a refreshing thought. She could see that Ed felt it too. The spell had been difficult. And how much truth was there to what R. L. said? Was it their actions that put them in this spot? What if they had just waited for Mom and Dad to come back when they were kidnapped?

"Ed?" Mel asked. "Have we unwittingly

been the problem?"

"Mel," Ed replied, "I think we have to revisit our intentions. If we have been preoccupied with catching R. L., we may have missed something."

Game to play: Decisions

Ed and Mel have a big decision to make. This decision will determine what their lives will look like from here on out. Play a game where the decision you make in the first move determines how you will play the rest of the game.

Materials needed:
- Game board and game cards. See Game Appendix.
- Optional: six-sided die for alternative rules.

Rules:
1. Each player will draw four cards, read the words, and figure out the prefix for each word.
    a. Each player will choose three cards to create a prefix pattern rule. They will place these cards in the desired order in the first three spaces on their game board.
    b. The prefix pattern rule determines the next card(s) that can be placed on the game board. The pattern must be followed, and it cannot be changed during the game.
    c. A player may choose to wait to place their prefix pattern rule cards until their next turn when they can draw an additional card to create a more desirable prefix pattern. If they want to wait for another turn after that, they may.
    d. Word cards that are not used in the prefix pattern rule will be saved in the player's "word bank."

e. Example: Player One draws these cards: misfit, prepay, redo, subway. They decide to make the prefix pattern mis-, sub-, re-. They will place the cards misfit, subway, and redo into the first three spaces on their game board in that order and place the card prepay to the side or in their word bank. Player Two draws these cards: retell, react, rerun, revisit. Since their only pattern choice is re-, re-, re-, and therefore the only words they could play must start with re-, they decide to wait to draw another card.

2. After the players have set their prefix pattern rule or decided to wait, Player One will draw and read one card before placing it in their word bank.

3. Player One will then place as many cards as they can from their word bank onto the game board. **The pattern rule must be followed and spaces cannot be skipped.** If Player One can't place a card for the next empty space, their turn is over.

4. It is now Player Two's turn.

5. The first player to reach the "End" on their game board wins the game.

Alternative Rules:

1. Player One draws a word, reads it, and then rolls a die.
   a. They can decide to move that many spaces on the game board OR
   b. Roll again to get a greater number. If they get a greater number, they can move that number of spaces, but if they get a lesser number, they lose their turn.

2. It is now Player Two's turn.

3. The first player to reach the "End" on their game board wins the game.

Chapter 10

Additional required skills for student text:

Ability to read words with the prefixes inter-, mid-, over-, and up-.

Barton Level: **Level 5 Lesson 10**.

Narrator (Parent or Tutor):

Since Ed and Mel hadn't slept since they arrived in Tashkent, they were extremely tired. It made it hard to think clearly. They were so close to helping the dragons, but maybe it was their fault that they were in trouble in the first place. If the dragons had never left Ebrin, then Ed, Mel, and Jax would have never had to craft the medicine. Jax would have never swum in front of Mel to save her from the jellyfish. Mel took a deep breath and put her head in her hands.

It would be so nice to get back to a pre-spell life, one that didn't have so much trouble and chaos. It felt like they were always working so hard. And now they had a chance to have the incurable spell actually removed. In fact, to get the spell removed they just had to walk away from a lot of their troubles. Maybe Ebrin would be better off without them.

Ed and Mel talked about how they could give the dragons the medicine, have the spell removed, and wait for their parents to join them. They could get back to traveling the world and seeing all the amazing people and cultures. They wouldn't have to study reading any more to regain their language abilities. They wouldn't have to think so hard to communicate their thoughts. They wouldn't be those kids under a spell anymore.

But somehow, even though it sounded wonderful and right to have the spell lifted, Ebrin had become a part of them. Running away now would be like running away from themselves. Even in their exhaustion, wisdom helped them remember.

The bigger picture was that the spell didn't define who they were, but it had helped them look to their strengths and problem solve in ways they wouldn't have done before. Who they were and how they dealt with the spell came from their character within. They valued truth, justice, family, and friends.

The bigger picture was that the Ebrin community was an amazing one like no other. Ed and Mel felt like they were home and not visitors when they were with the Ebrinites. Ebrin had become their home. How could they just walk away from that? But they had to accept that choosing Ebrin meant choosing to have the spell for the rest of their lives.

They also recognized that R. L. was working out of deceit and self-interest, even if it came from a place of hurt. They recognized that R. L. was trying to blame the consequences of his actions on them.

Ed and Mel wanted their decision to be made out of love for something and someone, not out of hurt from something or someone. They recognized the right thing to do wasn't necessarily the easy thing to do.

Ed and Mel decided they would never betray Ebrin, the dragons, Jax, or the values their parents had taught them. Ebrin had become their home. A spell could never take that away from them.

Suddenly the tent door opened and a tall figure walked in.

Student Text:

"We will not betray Ebrin!" Mel yelled as she anticipated R. L. wanting their answer.

"Um, O.K. How about I let you out of this pen, then?" It was Fred.

He added, "The baby dragons aren't doing well. You need to get them back to Ebrin. R. L. will not be happy, but I can't <u>watch</u> them get any sicker. The vet can't help, and there is nothing we can do to help them."

Fred unlocked the pen. "Quickly now, R. L. is on his way. Bree is waiting for you behind the tent," Fred said.

"Oh, thank you! We have meds for the

dragons! We will go to them now," Mel said.

"No, you will hand the meds to me," R. L. said as he stepped into the tent. "I will get them to the dragons. You were selfish not to tell me about the meds before.

"It looks like you two have chosen your path. It is upsetting that you didn't pick the option that was best for both of us. I'm afraid it doesn't end well for you now. I told you, I will do what I need to do to get what I want.

"And Fred, I am so upset with you. I am overwhelmed with your betrayal. How could you? After all I have done for you?"

Fred looked at R. L.'s feet, and then he gritted his teeth and said, "R. L., this is long overdue." Fred jumped on R. L., sending him to floor. Ed and Mel ran for the door, but R. L. upset the tent post. It landed on Mel's leg.

A few men ran into the tent and began pulling Fred off of R. L. Ed tried to lift the post off of Mel's leg, but R. L. grabbed her shoe. Ed began to combat R. L. Two men jumped on him.

Mel tried to run away. R. L. again grabbed her, and her bag flew open. Before she could cry out, one of the shots with the dragon's meds had been crushed.

As fast as the commotion had begun, it was over. The shot's toxin interacted with R. L.'s skin as it dripped from his hand.

Mel inched back from the broken glass. R. L. was motionless. R. L.'s eyes were blank as if he was unable to remember what he was doing or who he even was. R. L.'s men stopped to look at him.

"Um, Mel. Are you okay?" Ed said.

"I'm okay," Mel replied. "I think the hunt is over, Ed.

"R. L. grabbed the meds. It contacted his skin. His mind has been reset. I think it's blank. Remember the rat in the lab?"

Fred looked upset. "I just wanted you to

help the dragons. I didn't want to kill R. L.!"

"Don't overreact," Mel said. "It didn't kill him. It's his mind. He will have to be trained to do things again."

"Oh man, buddy. What did I do? I'll help him. I'll train him to walk and do things again, and I'll oversee other stuff too. He's not all bad. I'll help him be a respectable man," Fred said.

Bree stepped into the tent. "I'll help you, Fred. R. L. needs a few friends to help him. We all need some love to grow. But I have to say, if you have meds, Mel, the dragons need them right now."

Game to play: Intervention Race

Ed and Mel have stopped R. L. Nox, but they need to make it to the baby dragons to give them their medicine. Follow the path through the circus tents to get to the baby dragons.

Materials needed:
- Game board and game cards. See Game Appendix.
- Two game tokens.

Rules:
1. Player One draws and reads a card.
   a. If the word starts with the prefix "up-" they move their game token ahead one space.
   b. If the word starts with the prefix "inter-" they move their game token to the next intersection. If there are no more intersections ahead, move ahead one space.
   c. If the word starts with the prefix "mid-" they move their game token to the midpoint on the line they are on. If the midpoint is ahead of them, they move forward. If they have not reached the intersection and the midpoint is behind them, they move backwards. If they are already on the midpoint, they don't move.
   d. If the word starts with the prefix "over-" they move their game token ahead six spaces.
2. It is now Player Two's turn.
3. The first player to reach the "End" wins the game.

Chapter 11

Additional required skills for student text:

No new skills.

Barton Level: **No new lesson**.

Note: The word "home" is used out of order from the Barton scope and sequence.

Narrator (Parent or Tutor):

The baby dragons responded quickly to the medicine Mel made. Her careful attention to instructions, her skill in chemistry, and all the risks she, Ed, and Jax had taken paid off. The baby dragons were now safe from the toxin.

The risk. Mel thought of Jax. She was dying to know how he was doing. She couldn't wait to get back to Ebrin and find out.

Ed was talking with Fred and Bree when Mel joined them. They had already decided that Bree would indeed stay with Fred to help him with R. L. and with returning the stolen goods to Ebrin.

The dragons were starting to feel quite frisky, but the group felt the weight of the next problem they needed to solve. How were they going to get the dragons out of the circus unnoticed? Instead of sneaking the dragons out before the show started as planned, Ed and Mel had sat for hours in the lion pen. It was too late now to sneak them out. People were all over the place. There were lines at the concessions stands. There were lines at several of the bathrooms. Excited children were rushing to their seats, not wanting to miss a second. Teenagers wandered around with their friends, waiting to sit down just before the show started. Extra security officers were now working to help direct the crowds. It seemed impossible to get the dragons out unnoticed now.

Music filled the air. The dragons started jumping and tumbling with each other. The hustle and bustle were becoming overwhelming. Bree said to the dragons, "You two! You have to settle down. Everyone is going to be looking at you if you keep bouncing around like that."

Ed suddenly said, "That's it! We can't go into hiding, but we can put on a show!"

Fred responded, "I think you must have hit your head earlier, buddy. How can we hide the dragons if we have them go out in front of everyone?"

"All the people are expecting to see dragons in a show. If we go out there and put on a show, we can have a grand **EXIT**. They will expect us to **go** at the end. They will be thinking of traffic and getting to bed, and we will just walk away with the dragons," Ed said.

"I think that will actually work," said Fred. "I can get a truck. It won't matter if people see us loading the dragons into the truck after the show. I'll drive you around until we can get you to the metro station unnoticed."

It was decided. Bree, Ed, and Mel were going to join the dragons in a circus show the likes of which had never been seen before.

Indeed, the show was like no other. The audience was amazed at the dragons. They were so . . . realistic looking. The dragons rolled and played with Bree in the circus ring. They pounced on and attacked pumpkins like kittens attacking balls of yarn. They chased Ed and Mel around in a game that looked like tag. They even breathed their breath of fire at large ice sculptures to get a drink of water. After all, playing hard made them thirsty. The crowd went wild. Then Ed, Mel, and Bree took a bow and exited the main circus tent with the baby dragons.

As Ed, Mel, and the dragons were riding off in the van with Fred, the people leaving the circus talked about how realistic the dragons really were. Some said the dragons should have been meaner and more dangerous to make them more realistic. Some people, like a well-known vet from the area, insisted that the dragons were actually real. Most people laughed at that. The show had been amazing, but how could some people actually believe that dragons were real? Dragons were legend and myth, not reality. It was amazing to make believe for a little while, but almost everyone knew that dragons don't really exist.

But Fred and Bree knew the truth.

Ed and Mel knew too. And they had succeeded in protecting the baby dragons once again. They also knew that their grit, determination, and the support of their community had helped them succeed against the odds. They had stopped R. L., rescued the baby dragons, and saved Ebrin.

It was now time to return the dragons to Ebrin.

Student text:

"These baby dragons are still feeling a bit frisky," Mel said as they walked through the tunnel back to Ebrin. It had been a task getting the dragons down the subway steps and to the door to Ebrin, but they were successful without being seen.

"If you told me a year ago that I'd be walking baby dragons back to another land after we rescued them from a greedy man who we had to stop so he didn't demolish that land, well, I'd think that you had lost your mind," Ed said.

"Then if you added that was after we had to rescue our parents from this man who also put a spell on us, I would have been sure you had lost your mind."

"It does seem crazy. And look at you," Mel responded. "You are doing well with a dragon. You once were afraid of a cat or a dog."

Ed grinned and then stopped. "Mel, this is the end of the path."

Behind the door was the land and the people they had chosen over being free from the spell. Ed felt no regret.

"Ed, why did you stop?" Mel asked. "We've got to go see if Jax is okay. You're killing me. Get going!"

Ed and Mel stepped through the door.

A <u>watch</u>man greeted them and quickly ran to tell the others. Ed and Mel were back! They had the dragons!

Before long, a bunch of people met Ed and Mel. Mom and Dad were at the front with Ash. They hugged Ed and Mel.

Mel looked for Jax. "Mom, what about Jax? Is he—?" And then she spotted him.

Slowly, Jax was walking with the help of a walking stick to greet them. He had a grin as big as Texas.

Mel ran to Jax and hugged him.

"You did it," Jax whispered. "I'm glad you are back."

"I'm so happy to see you on your feet!"

Mel replied. "Are you going to be okay?"

Jax nodded yes. Ed met up with them. He was glad to see Jax and let out a laugh.

The rest of the day they spent celebrating and telling Mom, Dad, and Jax about all that had happened. They told them about Fred and Bree and their plans.

They were thankful that R. L.'s greed hadn't finished Ebrin or R. L. They were thankful that they had kept going even when the going had been tough.

That evening, they were thankful for the stunning green and gold sunset, and they were thankful for their new friends and <u>home</u>.

Epilogue

Narrator (Parent or Tutor):

The feeling that you are missing something. It can plague your dreams and hurt your confidence as it did Ed's.

Missing something. It can stand in your way as it did when Mel tried to use the science lab.

Missing something. It can defeat you as it did R. L. when he decided to steal Billy's lunch.

But there is hope.

Wisdom can help us see that maybe it isn't that we are missing something so much as we have room to grow personally and in community.

Ed could have quit, but he grew instead.

Mel could have quit, but she grew instead.

They could have fought R. L.'s greed on their own, but they worked with and became a part of a community instead.

Even R. L. has a chance to grow with a community to support him. Growing can be a messy or crazy process, but it is full of life and hope. May your journey be filled with growth, life, and hope.

Game to play: The Path's End

When one path ends, it is often good to take a look back before beginning a new path. A look back can help us see how much we have grown on the journey. That can give us courage as we look forward to new paths and all the growth that is needed to travel them. Read words from Barton level 3, level 4, and level 5 as you travel the game path.

Materials needed:
- Game board. See Game Appendix.
- Six-sided die.
- Game token for each player.

Rules:
1. Both players put their game tokens on "Start."
2. Player One rolls the die.
3. Player One moves their token the number of spaces rolled and reads the word on the game board.
4. It is now Player Two's turn.
5. The first player to the "End" wins.

Resource Appendix:

These web pages may provide encouragement and helpful information.

https://benfoss.com/make-dyslexia-about-strengths-not-shame/

https://www.psychologytoday.com/us/blog/worrier-warrior/201609/raising-dyslexic-kids-self-awareness-and-acceptance

https://sites.ed.gov/osers/2016/10/acceptance-achievement-because-of-my-dyslexia-not-in-spite-of-it/

Accommodation information:

https://www.dys-add.com/resources/General/AccommodationsHandout.pdf

https://www.dyslexicadvantage.org/self-advocacy-common-accommodations-and-modifications/

https://www.understood.org/en/learning-thinking-differences/treatments-approaches/educational-strategies/accommodations-what-they-are-and-how-they-work

Game Appendix:

NOTE: A PDF of the Game Appendix can be found at DecodableAdventures.com under the "eBook Users" page.

Also, check the "eBook Users" page for links to alternate digital formats for some games.

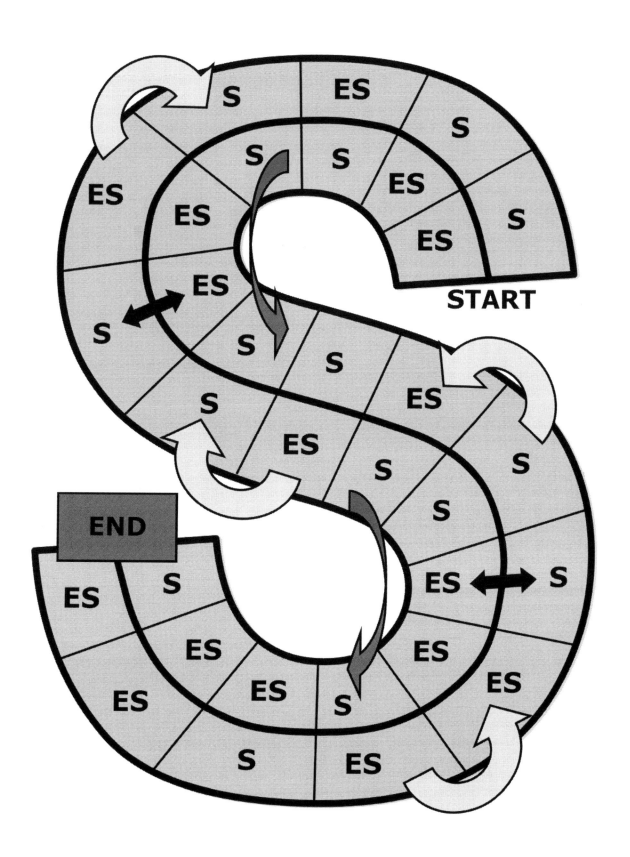

1 1 1 1 1 1 1 1 1 1 1 1 1 1 1 1 1 1 1 1 1 1 1 1 1 1 1 1 1 1 1 1 1 1 1 1 1 1 1 1
1 1 1 1 1 1 1 1 1 1 1 1 1 1 1 1 1 1 1 1 1 1 1 1 1 1 1 1 1 1 1 1 1 1 1 1 1 1 1 1
1 1 1 1 1 1 1 1 1 1 1 1 1 1 1 1 1 1 1 1 1 1 1 1 1 1 1 1 1 1 1 1 1 1 1 1 1 1 1 1
1 1 1 1 1 1 1 1 1 1 1 1 1 1 1 1 1 1 1 1 1 1 1 1 1 1 1 1 1 1 1 1 1 1 1 1 1 1 1 1
1 1 1 1 1 1 1 1 1 1 1 1 1 1 1 1 1 1 1 1 1 1 1 1 1 1 1 1 1 1 1 1 1 1 1 1 1 1 1 1
1 1 1 1 1 1 1 1 1 1 1 1 1 1 1 1 1 1 1 1 1 1 1 1 1 1 1 1 1 1 1 1 1 1 1 1 1 1 1 1
1 1 1 1 1 1 1 1 1 1 1 1 1 1 1 1 1 1 1 1 1 1 1 1 1 1 1 1 1 1 1 1 1 1 1 1 1 1 1 1
1 1 1 1 1 1 1 1 1 1 1 1 1 1 1 1 1 1 1 1 1 1 1 1 1 1 1 1 1 1 1 1 1 1 1 1 1 1 1 1
1 1 1 1 1 1 1 1 1 1 1 1 1 1 1 1 1 1 1 1 1 1 1 1 1 1 1 1 1 1 1 1 1 1 1 1 1 1 1 1
1 1 1 1 1 1 1 1 1 1 1 1 1 1 1 1 1 1 1 1 1 1 1 1 1 1 1 1 1 1 1 1 1 1 1 1 1 1 1 1
1 1 1 1 1 1 1 1 1 1 1 1 1 1 1 1 1 1 1 1 1 1 1 1 1 1 1 1 1 1 1 1 1 1 1 1 1 1 1 1
1 1 1 1 1 1 1 1 1 1 1 1 1 1 1 1 1 1 1 1 1 1 1 1 1 1 1 1 1 1 1 1 1 1 1 1 1 1 1 1
1 1 1 1 1 1 1 1 1 1 1 1 1 1 1 1 1 1 1 1 1 1 1 1 1 1 1 1 1 1 1 1 1 1 1 1 1 1 1 1
1 1 1 1 1 1 1 1 1 1 1 1 1 1 1 1 1 1 1 1 1 1 1 1 1 1 1 1 1 1 1 1 1 1 1 1 1 1 1 1
1 1 1 1 1 1 1 1 1 1 1 1 1 1 1 1 1 1 1 1 1 1 1 1 1 1 1 1 1 1 1 1 1 1 1 1 1 1 1 1
1 1 1 1 1 1 1 1 1 1 1 1 1 1 1 1 1 1 1 1 1 1 1 1 1 1 1 1 1 1 1 1 1 1 1 1 1 1 1 1
1 1 1 1 1 1 1 1 1 1 1 1 1 1 1 1 1 1 1 1 1 1 1 1 1 1 1 1 1 1 1 1 1 1 1 1 1 1 1 1
1 1 1 1 1 1 1 1 1 1 1 1 1 1 1 1 1 1 1 1 1 1 1 1 1 1 1 1 1 1 1 1 1 1 1 1 1 1 1 1
1 1 1 1 1 1 1 1 1 1 1 1 1 1 1 1 1 1 1 1 1 1 1 1 1 1 1 1 1 1 1 1 1 1 1 1 1 1 1 1
1 1 1 1 1 1 1 1 1 1 1 1 1 1 1 1 1 1 1 1 1 1 1 1 1 1 1 1 1 1 1 1 1 1 1 1 1 1 1 1
1 1 1 1 1 1 1 1 1 1 1 1 1 1 1 1 1 1 1 1 1 1 1 1 1 1 1 1 1 1 1 1 1 1 1 1 1 1 1 1
1 1 1 1 1 1 1 1 1 1 1 1 1 1 1 1 1 1 1 1 1 1 1 1 1 1 1 1 1 1 1 1 1 1 1 1 1 1 1 1
1 1 1 1 1 1 1 1 1 1 1 1 1 1 1 1 1 1 1 1 1 1 1 1 1 1 1 1 1 1 1 1 1 1 1 1 1 1 1 1
1 1 1 1 1 1 1 1 1 1 1 1 1 1 1 1 1 1 1 1 1 1 1 1 1 1 1 1 1 1 1 1 1 1 1 1 1 1 1 1
1 1 1 1 1 1 1 1 1 1 1 1 1 1 1 1 1 1 1 1 1 1 1 1 1 1 1 1 1 1 1 1 1 1 1 1 1 1 1 1
1 1 1 1 1 1 1 1 1 1 1 1 1 1 1 1 1 1 1 1 1 1 1 1 1 1 1 1 1 1 1 1 1 1 1 1 1 1 1 1
1 1 1 1 1 1 1 1 1 1 1 1 1 1 1 1 1 1 1 1 1 1 1 1 1 1 1 1 1 1 1 1 1 1 1 1 1 1 1 1
1 1 1 1 1 1 1 1 1 1 1 1 1 1 1 1 1 1 1 1 1 1 1 1 1 1 1 1 1 1 1 1 1 1 1 1 1 1 1 1
1 1 1 1 1 1 1 1 1 1 1 1 1 1 1 1 1 1 1 1 1 1 1 1 1 1 1 1 1 1 1 1 1 1 1 1 1 1 1 1
1 1 1 1 1 1 1 1 1 1 1 1 1 1 1 1 1 1 1 1 1 1 1 1 1 1 1 1 1 1 1 1 1 1 1 1 1 1 1 1
1 1 1 1 1 1 1 1 1 1 1 1 1 1 1 1 1 1 1 1 1 1 1 1 1 1 1 1 1 1 1 1 1 1 1 1 1 1 1 1
1 1 1 1 1 1 1 1 1 1 1 1 1 1 1 1 1 1 1 1 1 1 1 1 1 1 1 1 1 1 1 1 1 1 1 1 1 1 1 1
1 1 1 1 1 1 1 1 1 1 1 1 1 1 1 1 1 1 1 1 1 1 1 1 1 1 1 1 1 1 1 1 1 1 1 1 1 1 1 1

insects	shops	dragons	meds
things	elements	tents	days
components	hugs	kids	sleeps
shows	streets	plants	songs
clues	rugs	folds	spots

1 1 1 1 1 1 1 1 1 1 1 1 1 1 1 1 1 1 1 1 1 1 1 1 1 1 1 1 1 1 1 1 1
1 1 1 1 1 1 1 1 1 1 1 1 1 1 1 1 1 1 1 1 1 1 1 1 1 1 1 1 1 1 1 1 1
1 1 1 1 1 1 1 1 1 1 1 1 1 1 1 1 1 1 1 1 1 1 1 1 1 1 1 1 1 1 1 1 1
1 1 1 1 1 1 1 1 1 1 1 1 1 1 1 1 1 1 1 1 1 1 1 1 1 1 1 1 1 1 1 1 1
1 1 1 1 1 1 1 1 1 1 1 1 1 1 1 1 1 1 1 1 1 1 1 1 1 1 1 1 1 1 1 1 1
1 1 1 1 1 1 1 1 1 1 1 1 1 1 1 1 1 1 1 1 1 1 1 1 1 1 1 1 1 1 1 1 1
1 1 1 1 1 1 1 1 1 1 1 1 1 1 1 1 1 1 1 1 1 1 1 1 1 1 1 1 1 1 1 1 1
1 1 1 1 1 1 1 1 1 1 1 1 1 1 1 1 1 1 1 1 1 1 1 1 1 1 1 1 1 1 1 1 1
1 1 1 1 1 1 1 1 1 1 1 1 1 1 1 1 1 1 1 1 1 1 1 1 1 1 1 1 1 1 1 1 1
1 1 1 1 1 1 1 1 1 1 1 1 1 1 1 1 1 1 1 1 1 1 1 1 1 1 1 1 1 1 1 1 1
1 1 1 1 1 1 1 1 1 1 1 1 1 1 1 1 1 1 1 1 1 1 1 1 1 1 1 1 1 1 1 1 1
1 1 1 1 1 1 1 1 1 1 1 1 1 1 1 1 1 1 1 1 1 1 1 1 1 1 1 1 1 1 1 1 1
1 1 1 1 1 1 1 1 1 1 1 1 1 1 1 1 1 1 1 1 1 1 1 1 1 1 1 1 1 1 1 1 1
1 1 1 1 1 1 1 1 1 1 1 1 1 1 1 1 1 1 1 1 1 1 1 1 1 1 1 1 1 1 1 1 1
1 1 1 1 1 1 1 1 1 1 1 1 1 1 1 1 1 1 1 1 1 1 1 1 1 1 1 1 1 1 1 1 1
1 1 1 1 1 1 1 1 1 1 1 1 1 1 1 1 1 1 1 1 1 1 1 1 1 1 1 1 1 1 1 1 1
1 1 1 1 1 1 1 1 1 1 1 1 1 1 1 1 1 1 1 1 1 1 1 1 1 1 1 1 1 1 1 1 1
1 1 1 1 1 1 1 1 1 1 1 1 1 1 1 1 1 1 1 1 1 1 1 1 1 1 1 1 1 1 1 1 1
1 1 1 1 1 1 1 1 1 1 1 1 1 1 1 1 1 1 1 1 1 1 1 1 1 1 1 1 1 1 1 1 1
1 1 1 1 1 1 1 1 1 1 1 1 1 1 1 1 1 1 1 1 1 1 1 1 1 1 1 1 1 1 1 1 1
1 1 1 1 1 1 1 1 1 1 1 1 1 1 1 1 1 1 1 1 1 1 1 1 1 1 1 1 1 1 1 1 1
1 1 1 1 1 1 1 1 1 1 1 1 1 1 1 1 1 1 1 1 1 1 1 1 1 1 1 1 1 1 1 1 1
1 1 1 1 1 1 1 1 1 1 1 1 1 1 1 1 1 1 1 1 1 1 1 1 1 1 1 1 1 1 1 1 1
1 1 1 1 1 1 1 1 1 1 1 1 1 1 1 1 1 1 1 1 1 1 1 1 1 1 1 1 1 1 1 1 1
1 1 1 1 1 1 1 1 1 1 1 1 1 1 1 1 1 1 1 1 1 1 1 1 1 1 1 1 1 1 1 1 1
1 1 1 1 1 1 1 1 1 1 1 1 1 1 1 1 1 1 1 1 1 1 1 1 1 1 1 1 1 1 1 1 1
1 1 1 1 1 1 1 1 1 1 1 1 1 1 1 1 1 1 1 1 1 1 1 1 1 1 1 1 1 1 1 1 1
1 1 1 1 1 1 1 1 1 1 1 1 1 1 1 1 1 1 1 1 1 1 1 1 1 1 1 1 1 1 1 1 1
1 1 1 1 1 1 1 1 1 1 1 1 1 1 1 1 1 1 1 1 1 1 1 1 1 1 1 1 1 1 1 1 1
1 1 1 1 1 1 1 1 1 1 1 1 1 1 1 1 1 1 1 1 1 1 1 1 1 1 1 1 1 1 1 1 1
1 1 1 1 1 1 1 1 1 1 1 1 1 1 1 1 1 1 1 1 1 1 1 1 1 1 1 1 1 1 1 1 1
1 1 1 1 1 1 1 1 1 1 1 1 1 1 1 1 1 1 1 1 1 1 1 1 1 1 1 1 1 1 1 1 1

boxes	bunches	lunches	ashes
kisses	classes	dishes	losses
scratches	buzzes	grasses	itches
ditches	vetoes	fixes	heroes
fails	brews	hours	rescues

1 1 1 1 1 1 1 1 1 1 1 1 1 1 1 1 1 1 1 1 1 1 1 1 1 1 1 1 1 1 1 1 1 1 1 1 1 1 1 1 1 1 1 1
1 1 1 1 1 1 1 1 1 1 1 1 1 1 1 1 1 1 1 1 1 1 1 1 1 1 1 1 1 1 1 1 1 1 1 1 1 1 1 1 1 1 1 1
1 1 1 1 1 1 1 1 1 1 1 1 1 1 1 1 1 1 1 1 1 1 1 1 1 1 1 1 1 1 1 1 1 1 1 1 1 1 1 1 1 1 1 1
1 1 1 1 1 1 1 1 1 1 1 1 1 1 1 1 1 1 1 1 1 1 1 1 1 1 1 1 1 1 1 1 1 1 1 1 1 1 1 1 1 1 1 1
1 1 1 1 1 1 1 1 1 1 1 1 1 1 1 1 1 1 1 1 1 1 1 1 1 1 1 1 1 1 1 1 1 1 1 1 1 1 1 1 1 1 1 1
1 1 1 1 1 1 1 1 1 1 1 1 1 1 1 1 1 1 1 1 1 1 1 1 1 1 1 1 1 1 1 1 1 1 1 1 1 1 1 1 1 1 1 1
1 1 1 1 1 1 1 1 1 1 1 1 1 1 1 1 1 1 1 1 1 1 1 1 1 1 1 1 1 1 1 1 1 1 1 1 1 1 1 1 1 1 1 1
1 1 1 1 1 1 1 1 1 1 1 1 1 1 1 1 1 1 1 1 1 1 1 1 1 1 1 1 1 1 1 1 1 1 1 1 1 1 1 1 1 1 1 1
1 1 1 1 1 1 1 1 1 1 1 1 1 1 1 1 1 1 1 1 1 1 1 1 1 1 1 1 1 1 1 1 1 1 1 1 1 1 1 1 1 1 1 1
1 1 1 1 1 1 1 1 1 1 1 1 1 1 1 1 1 1 1 1 1 1 1 1 1 1 1 1 1 1 1 1 1 1 1 1 1 1 1 1 1 1 1 1
1 1 1 1 1 1 1 1 1 1 1 1 1 1 1 1 1 1 1 1 1 1 1 1 1 1 1 1 1 1 1 1 1 1 1 1 1 1 1 1 1 1 1 1
1 1 1 1 1 1 1 1 1 1 1 1 1 1 1 1 1 1 1 1 1 1 1 1 1 1 1 1 1 1 1 1 1 1 1 1 1 1 1 1 1 1 1 1
1 1 1 1 1 1 1 1 1 1 1 1 1 1 1 1 1 1 1 1 1 1 1 1 1 1 1 1 1 1 1 1 1 1 1 1 1 1 1 1 1 1 1 1
1 1 1 1 1 1 1 1 1 1 1 1 1 1 1 1 1 1 1 1 1 1 1 1 1 1 1 1 1 1 1 1 1 1 1 1 1 1 1 1 1 1 1 1
1 1 1 1 1 1 1 1 1 1 1 1 1 1 1 1 1 1 1 1 1 1 1 1 1 1 1 1 1 1 1 1 1 1 1 1 1 1 1 1 1 1 1 1
1 1 1 1 1 1 1 1 1 1 1 1 1 1 1 1 1 1 1 1 1 1 1 1 1 1 1 1 1 1 1 1 1 1 1 1 1 1 1 1 1 1 1 1
1 1 1 1 1 1 1 1 1 1 1 1 1 1 1 1 1 1 1 1 1 1 1 1 1 1 1 1 1 1 1 1 1 1 1 1 1 1 1 1 1 1 1 1
1 1 1 1 1 1 1 1 1 1 1 1 1 1 1 1 1 1 1 1 1 1 1 1 1 1 1 1 1 1 1 1 1 1 1 1 1 1 1 1 1 1 1 1
1 1 1 1 1 1 1 1 1 1 1 1 1 1 1 1 1 1 1 1 1 1 1 1 1 1 1 1 1 1 1 1 1 1 1 1 1 1 1 1 1 1 1 1
1 1 1 1 1 1 1 1 1 1 1 1 1 1 1 1 1 1 1 1 1 1 1 1 1 1 1 1 1 1 1 1 1 1 1 1 1 1 1 1 1 1 1 1
1 1 1 1 1 1 1 1 1 1 1 1 1 1 1 1 1 1 1 1 1 1 1 1 1 1 1 1 1 1 1 1 1 1 1 1 1 1 1 1 1 1 1 1
1 1 1 1 1 1 1 1 1 1 1 1 1 1 1 1 1 1 1 1 1 1 1 1 1 1 1 1 1 1 1 1 1 1 1 1 1 1 1 1 1 1 1 1
1 1 1 1 1 1 1 1 1 1 1 1 1 1 1 1 1 1 1 1 1 1 1 1 1 1 1 1 1 1 1 1 1 1 1 1 1 1 1 1 1 1 1 1
1 1 1 1 1 1 1 1 1 1 1 1 1 1 1 1 1 1 1 1 1 1 1 1 1 1 1 1 1 1 1 1 1 1 1 1 1 1 1 1 1 1 1 1
1 1 1 1 1 1 1 1 1 1 1 1 1 1 1 1 1 1 1 1 1 1 1 1 1 1 1 1 1 1 1 1 1 1 1 1 1 1 1 1 1 1 1 1
1 1 1 1 1 1 1 1 1 1 1 1 1 1 1 1 1 1 1 1 1 1 1 1 1 1 1 1 1 1 1 1 1 1 1 1 1 1 1 1 1 1 1 1
1 1 1 1 1 1 1 1 1 1 1 1 1 1 1 1 1 1 1 1 1 1 1 1 1 1 1 1 1 1 1 1 1 1 1 1 1 1 1 1 1 1 1 1
1 1 1 1 1 1 1 1 1 1 1 1 1 1 1 1 1 1 1 1 1 1 1 1 1 1 1 1 1 1 1 1 1 1 1 1 1 1 1 1 1 1 1 1
1 1 1 1 1 1 1 1 1 1 1 1 1 1 1 1 1 1 1 1 1 1 1 1 1 1 1 1 1 1 1 1 1 1 1 1 1 1 1 1 1 1 1 1
1 1 1 1 1 1 1 1 1 1 1 1 1 1 1 1 1 1 1 1 1 1 1 1 1 1 1 1 1 1 1 1 1 1 1 1 1 1 1 1 1 1 1 1
1 1 1 1 1 1 1 1 1 1 1 1 1 1 1 1 1 1 1 1 1 1 1 1 1 1 1 1 1 1 1 1 1 1 1 1 1 1 1 1 1 1 1 1
1 1 1 1 1 1 1 1 1 1 1 1 1 1 1 1 1 1 1 1 1 1 1 1 1 1 1 1 1 1 1 1 1 1 1 1 1 1 1 1 1 1 1 1
1 1 1 1 1 1 1 1 1 1 1 1 1 1 1 1 1 1 1 1 1 1 1 1 1 1 1 1 1 1 1 1 1 1 1 1 1 1 1 1 1 1 1 1

ful	ly	less
ful	ly	less
ful	ly	less

2 2 2 2 2 2 2 2 2 2 2 2 2 2 2 2 2 2 2 2 2 2 2 2 2 2 2 2 2 2 2 2 2 2 2 2 2 2 2 2
2 2 2 2 2 2 2 2 2 2 2 2 2 2 2 2 2 2 2 2 2 2 2 2 2 2 2 2 2 2 2 2 2 2 2 2 2 2 2 2
2 2 2 2 2 2 2 2 2 2 2 2 2 2 2 2 2 2 2 2 2 2 2 2 2 2 2 2 2 2 2 2 2 2 2 2 2 2 2 2
2 2 2 2 2 2 2 2 2 2 2 2 2 2 2 2 2 2 2 2 2 2 2 2 2 2 2 2 2 2 2 2 2 2 2 2 2 2 2 2
2 2 2 2 2 2 2 2 2 2 2 2 2 2 2 2 2 2 2 2 2 2 2 2 2 2 2 2 2 2 2 2 2 2 2 2 2 2 2 2
2 2 2 2 2 2 2 2 2 2 2 2 2 2 2 2 2 2 2 2 2 2 2 2 2 2 2 2 2 2 2 2 2 2 2 2 2 2 2 2
2 2 2 2 2 2 2 2 2 2 2 2 2 2 2 2 2 2 2 2 2 2 2 2 2 2 2 2 2 2 2 2 2 2 2 2 2 2 2 2
2 2 2 2 2 2 2 2 2 2 2 2 2 2 2 2 2 2 2 2 2 2 2 2 2 2 2 2 2 2 2 2 2 2 2 2 2 2 2 2
2 2 2 2 2 2 2 2 2 2 2 2 2 2 2 2 2 2 2 2 2 2 2 2 2 2 2 2 2 2 2 2 2 2 2 2 2 2 2 2
2 2 2 2 2 2 2 2 2 2 2 2 2 2 2 2 2 2 2 2 2 2 2 2 2 2 2 2 2 2 2 2 2 2 2 2 2 2 2 2
2 2 2 2 2 2 2 2 2 2 2 2 2 2 2 2 2 2 2 2 2 2 2 2 2 2 2 2 2 2 2 2 2 2 2 2 2 2 2 2
2 2 2 2 2 2 2 2 2 2 2 2 2 2 2 2 2 2 2 2 2 2 2 2 2 2 2 2 2 2 2 2 2 2 2 2 2 2 2 2
2 2 2 2 2 2 2 2 2 2 2 2 2 2 2 2 2 2 2 2 2 2 2 2 2 2 2 2 2 2 2 2 2 2 2 2 2 2 2 2
2 2 2 2 2 2 2 2 2 2 2 2 2 2 2 2 2 2 2 2 2 2 2 2 2 2 2 2 2 2 2 2 2 2 2 2 2 2 2 2
2 2 2 2 2 2 2 2 2 2 2 2 2 2 2 2 2 2 2 2 2 2 2 2 2 2 2 2 2 2 2 2 2 2 2 2 2 2 2 2
2 2 2 2 2 2 2 2 2 2 2 2 2 2 2 2 2 2 2 2 2 2 2 2 2 2 2 2 2 2 2 2 2 2 2 2 2 2 2 2
2 2 2 2 2 2 2 2 2 2 2 2 2 2 2 2 2 2 2 2 2 2 2 2 2 2 2 2 2 2 2 2 2 2 2 2 2 2 2 2
2 2 2 2 2 2 2 2 2 2 2 2 2 2 2 2 2 2 2 2 2 2 2 2 2 2 2 2 2 2 2 2 2 2 2 2 2 2 2 2
2 2 2 2 2 2 2 2 2 2 2 2 2 2 2 2 2 2 2 2 2 2 2 2 2 2 2 2 2 2 2 2 2 2 2 2 2 2 2 2
2 2 2 2 2 2 2 2 2 2 2 2 2 2 2 2 2 2 2 2 2 2 2 2 2 2 2 2 2 2 2 2 2 2 2 2 2 2 2 2
2 2 2 2 2 2 2 2 2 2 2 2 2 2 2 2 2 2 2 2 2 2 2 2 2 2 2 2 2 2 2 2 2 2 2 2 2 2 2 2
2 2 2 2 2 2 2 2 2 2 2 2 2 2 2 2 2 2 2 2 2 2 2 2 2 2 2 2 2 2 2 2 2 2 2 2 2 2 2 2
2 2 2 2 2 2 2 2 2 2 2 2 2 2 2 2 2 2 2 2 2 2 2 2 2 2 2 2 2 2 2 2 2 2 2 2 2 2 2 2
2 2 2 2 2 2 2 2 2 2 2 2 2 2 2 2 2 2 2 2 2 2 2 2 2 2 2 2 2 2 2 2 2 2 2 2 2 2 2 2
2 2 2 2 2 2 2 2 2 2 2 2 2 2 2 2 2 2 2 2 2 2 2 2 2 2 2 2 2 2 2 2 2 2 2 2 2 2 2 2
2 2 2 2 2 2 2 2 2 2 2 2 2 2 2 2 2 2 2 2 2 2 2 2 2 2 2 2 2 2 2 2 2 2 2 2 2 2 2 2
2 2 2 2 2 2 2 2 2 2 2 2 2 2 2 2 2 2 2 2 2 2 2 2 2 2 2 2 2 2 2 2 2 2 2 2 2 2 2 2
2 2 2 2 2 2 2 2 2 2 2 2 2 2 2 2 2 2 2 2 2 2 2 2 2 2 2 2 2 2 2 2 2 2 2 2 2 2 2 2
2 2 2 2 2 2 2 2 2 2 2 2 2 2 2 2 2 2 2 2 2 2 2 2 2 2 2 2 2 2 2 2 2 2 2 2 2 2 2 2
2 2 2 2 2 2 2 2 2 2 2 2 2 2 2 2 2 2 2 2 2 2 2 2 2 2 2 2 2 2 2 2 2 2 2 2 2 2 2 2
2 2 2 2 2 2 2 2 2 2 2 2 2 2 2 2 2 2 2 2 2 2 2 2 2 2 2 2 2 2 2 2 2 2 2 2 2 2 2 2
2 2 2 2 2 2 2 2 2 2 2 2 2 2 2 2 2 2 2 2 2 2 2 2 2 2 2 2 2 2 2 2 2 2 2 2 2 2 2 2

ful	ly	less
ful	ly	less
ful	ly	less

2 2 2 2 2 2 2 2 2 2 2 2 2 2 2 2 2 2 2 2 2 2 2 2 2 2 2 2 2 2
2 2 2 2 2 2 2 2 2 2 2 2 2 2 2 2 2 2 2 2 2 2 2 2 2 2 2 2 2 2
2 2 2 2 2 2 2 2 2 2 2 2 2 2 2 2 2 2 2 2 2 2 2 2 2 2 2 2 2 2
2 2 2 2 2 2 2 2 2 2 2 2 2 2 2 2 2 2 2 2 2 2 2 2 2 2 2 2 2 2
2 2 2 2 2 2 2 2 2 2 2 2 2 2 2 2 2 2 2 2 2 2 2 2 2 2 2 2 2 2
2 2 2 2 2 2 2 2 2 2 2 2 2 2 2 2 2 2 2 2 2 2 2 2 2 2 2 2 2 2
2 2 2 2 2 2 2 2 2 2 2 2 2 2 2 2 2 2 2 2 2 2 2 2 2 2 2 2 2 2
2 2 2 2 2 2 2 2 2 2 2 2 2 2 2 2 2 2 2 2 2 2 2 2 2 2 2 2 2 2
2 2 2 2 2 2 2 2 2 2 2 2 2 2 2 2 2 2 2 2 2 2 2 2 2 2 2 2 2 2
2 2 2 2 2 2 2 2 2 2 2 2 2 2 2 2 2 2 2 2 2 2 2 2 2 2 2 2 2 2
2 2 2 2 2 2 2 2 2 2 2 2 2 2 2 2 2 2 2 2 2 2 2 2 2 2 2 2 2 2
2 2 2 2 2 2 2 2 2 2 2 2 2 2 2 2 2 2 2 2 2 2 2 2 2 2 2 2 2 2
2 2 2 2 2 2 2 2 2 2 2 2 2 2 2 2 2 2 2 2 2 2 2 2 2 2 2 2 2 2
2 2 2 2 2 2 2 2 2 2 2 2 2 2 2 2 2 2 2 2 2 2 2 2 2 2 2 2 2 2
2 2 2 2 2 2 2 2 2 2 2 2 2 2 2 2 2 2 2 2 2 2 2 2 2 2 2 2 2 2
2 2 2 2 2 2 2 2 2 2 2 2 2 2 2 2 2 2 2 2 2 2 2 2 2 2 2 2 2 2
2 2 2 2 2 2 2 2 2 2 2 2 2 2 2 2 2 2 2 2 2 2 2 2 2 2 2 2 2 2
2 2 2 2 2 2 2 2 2 2 2 2 2 2 2 2 2 2 2 2 2 2 2 2 2 2 2 2 2 2
2 2 2 2 2 2 2 2 2 2 2 2 2 2 2 2 2 2 2 2 2 2 2 2 2 2 2 2 2 2
2 2 2 2 2 2 2 2 2 2 2 2 2 2 2 2 2 2 2 2 2 2 2 2 2 2 2 2 2 2
2 2 2 2 2 2 2 2 2 2 2 2 2 2 2 2 2 2 2 2 2 2 2 2 2 2 2 2 2 2
2 2 2 2 2 2 2 2 2 2 2 2 2 2 2 2 2 2 2 2 2 2 2 2 2 2 2 2 2 2
2 2 2 2 2 2 2 2 2 2 2 2 2 2 2 2 2 2 2 2 2 2 2 2 2 2 2 2 2 2
2 2 2 2 2 2 2 2 2 2 2 2 2 2 2 2 2 2 2 2 2 2 2 2 2 2 2 2 2 2
2 2 2 2 2 2 2 2 2 2 2 2 2 2 2 2 2 2 2 2 2 2 2 2 2 2 2 2 2 2
2 2 2 2 2 2 2 2 2 2 2 2 2 2 2 2 2 2 2 2 2 2 2 2 2 2 2 2 2 2
2 2 2 2 2 2 2 2 2 2 2 2 2 2 2 2 2 2 2 2 2 2 2 2 2 2 2 2 2 2
2 2 2 2 2 2 2 2 2 2 2 2 2 2 2 2 2 2 2 2 2 2 2 2 2 2 2 2 2 2
2 2 2 2 2 2 2 2 2 2 2 2 2 2 2 2 2 2 2 2 2 2 2 2 2 2 2 2 2 2
2 2 2 2 2 2 2 2 2 2 2 2 2 2 2 2 2 2 2 2 2 2 2 2 2 2 2 2 2 2
2 2 2 2 2 2 2 2 2 2 2 2 2 2 2 2 2 2 2 2 2 2 2 2 2 2 2 2 2 2
2 2 2 2 2 2 2 2 2 2 2 2 2 2 2 2 2 2 2 2 2 2 2 2 2 2 2 2 2 2
2 2 2 2 2 2 2 2 2 2 2 2 2 2 2 2 2 2 2 2 2 2 2 2 2 2 2 2 2 2

ful	ly	less
ful	ly	less
ness	ness	ness

2 2 2 2 2 2 2 2 2 2 2 2 2 2 2 2 2 2 2 2 2 2 2 2 2 2 2 2 2 2 2 2 2 2 2 2 2 2 2 2 2 2 2 2 2
2 2 2 2 2 2 2 2 2 2 2 2 2 2 2 2 2 2 2 2 2 2 2 2 2 2 2 2 2 2 2 2 2 2 2 2 2 2 2 2 2 2 2 2 2
2 2 2 2 2 2 2 2 2 2 2 2 2 2 2 2 2 2 2 2 2 2 2 2 2 2 2 2 2 2 2 2 2 2 2 2 2 2 2 2 2 2 2 2 2
2 2 2 2 2 2 2 2 2 2 2 2 2 2 2 2 2 2 2 2 2 2 2 2 2 2 2 2 2 2 2 2 2 2 2 2 2 2 2 2 2 2 2 2 2
2 2 2 2 2 2 2 2 2 2 2 2 2 2 2 2 2 2 2 2 2 2 2 2 2 2 2 2 2 2 2 2 2 2 2 2 2 2 2 2 2 2 2 2 2
2 2 2 2 2 2 2 2 2 2 2 2 2 2 2 2 2 2 2 2 2 2 2 2 2 2 2 2 2 2 2 2 2 2 2 2 2 2 2 2 2 2 2 2 2
2 2 2 2 2 2 2 2 2 2 2 2 2 2 2 2 2 2 2 2 2 2 2 2 2 2 2 2 2 2 2 2 2 2 2 2 2 2 2 2 2 2 2 2 2
2 2 2 2 2 2 2 2 2 2 2 2 2 2 2 2 2 2 2 2 2 2 2 2 2 2 2 2 2 2 2 2 2 2 2 2 2 2 2 2 2 2 2 2 2
2 2 2 2 2 2 2 2 2 2 2 2 2 2 2 2 2 2 2 2 2 2 2 2 2 2 2 2 2 2 2 2 2 2 2 2 2 2 2 2 2 2 2 2 2
2 2 2 2 2 2 2 2 2 2 2 2 2 2 2 2 2 2 2 2 2 2 2 2 2 2 2 2 2 2 2 2 2 2 2 2 2 2 2 2 2 2 2 2 2
2 2 2 2 2 2 2 2 2 2 2 2 2 2 2 2 2 2 2 2 2 2 2 2 2 2 2 2 2 2 2 2 2 2 2 2 2 2 2 2 2 2 2 2 2
2 2 2 2 2 2 2 2 2 2 2 2 2 2 2 2 2 2 2 2 2 2 2 2 2 2 2 2 2 2 2 2 2 2 2 2 2 2 2 2 2 2 2 2 2
2 2 2 2 2 2 2 2 2 2 2 2 2 2 2 2 2 2 2 2 2 2 2 2 2 2 2 2 2 2 2 2 2 2 2 2 2 2 2 2 2 2 2 2 2
2 2 2 2 2 2 2 2 2 2 2 2 2 2 2 2 2 2 2 2 2 2 2 2 2 2 2 2 2 2 2 2 2 2 2 2 2 2 2 2 2 2 2 2 2
2 2 2 2 2 2 2 2 2 2 2 2 2 2 2 2 2 2 2 2 2 2 2 2 2 2 2 2 2 2 2 2 2 2 2 2 2 2 2 2 2 2 2 2 2
2 2 2 2 2 2 2 2 2 2 2 2 2 2 2 2 2 2 2 2 2 2 2 2 2 2 2 2 2 2 2 2 2 2 2 2 2 2 2 2 2 2 2 2 2
2 2 2 2 2 2 2 2 2 2 2 2 2 2 2 2 2 2 2 2 2 2 2 2 2 2 2 2 2 2 2 2 2 2 2 2 2 2 2 2 2 2 2 2 2
2 2 2 2 2 2 2 2 2 2 2 2 2 2 2 2 2 2 2 2 2 2 2 2 2 2 2 2 2 2 2 2 2 2 2 2 2 2 2 2 2 2 2 2 2
2 2 2 2 2 2 2 2 2 2 2 2 2 2 2 2 2 2 2 2 2 2 2 2 2 2 2 2 2 2 2 2 2 2 2 2 2 2 2 2 2 2 2 2 2
2 2 2 2 2 2 2 2 2 2 2 2 2 2 2 2 2 2 2 2 2 2 2 2 2 2 2 2 2 2 2 2 2 2 2 2 2 2 2 2 2 2 2 2 2
2 2 2 2 2 2 2 2 2 2 2 2 2 2 2 2 2 2 2 2 2 2 2 2 2 2 2 2 2 2 2 2 2 2 2 2 2 2 2 2 2 2 2 2 2
2 2 2 2 2 2 2 2 2 2 2 2 2 2 2 2 2 2 2 2 2 2 2 2 2 2 2 2 2 2 2 2 2 2 2 2 2 2 2 2 2 2 2 2 2
2 2 2 2 2 2 2 2 2 2 2 2 2 2 2 2 2 2 2 2 2 2 2 2 2 2 2 2 2 2 2 2 2 2 2 2 2 2 2 2 2 2 2 2 2
2 2 2 2 2 2 2 2 2 2 2 2 2 2 2 2 2 2 2 2 2 2 2 2 2 2 2 2 2 2 2 2 2 2 2 2 2 2 2 2 2 2 2 2 2
2 2 2 2 2 2 2 2 2 2 2 2 2 2 2 2 2 2 2 2 2 2 2 2 2 2 2 2 2 2 2 2 2 2 2 2 2 2 2 2 2 2 2 2 2
2 2 2 2 2 2 2 2 2 2 2 2 2 2 2 2 2 2 2 2 2 2 2 2 2 2 2 2 2 2 2 2 2 2 2 2 2 2 2 2 2 2 2 2 2
2 2 2 2 2 2 2 2 2 2 2 2 2 2 2 2 2 2 2 2 2 2 2 2 2 2 2 2 2 2 2 2 2 2 2 2 2 2 2 2 2 2 2 2 2
2 2 2 2 2 2 2 2 2 2 2 2 2 2 2 2 2 2 2 2 2 2 2 2 2 2 2 2 2 2 2 2 2 2 2 2 2 2 2 2 2 2 2 2 2
2 2 2 2 2 2 2 2 2 2 2 2 2 2 2 2 2 2 2 2 2 2 2 2 2 2 2 2 2 2 2 2 2 2 2 2 2 2 2 2 2 2 2 2 2
2 2 2 2 2 2 2 2 2 2 2 2 2 2 2 2 2 2 2 2 2 2 2 2 2 2 2 2 2 2 2 2 2 2 2 2 2 2 2 2 2 2 2 2 2
2 2 2 2 2 2 2 2 2 2 2 2 2 2 2 2 2 2 2 2 2 2 2 2 2 2 2 2 2 2 2 2 2 2 2 2 2 2 2 2 2 2 2 2 2
2 2 2 2 2 2 2 2 2 2 2 2 2 2 2 2 2 2 2 2 2 2 2 2 2 2 2 2 2 2 2 2 2 2 2 2 2 2 2 2 2 2 2 2 2
2 2 2 2 2 2 2 2 2 2 2 2 2 2 2 2 2 2 2 2 2 2 2 2 2 2 2 2 2 2 2 2 2 2 2 2 2 2 2 2 2 2 2 2 2

ness	ness	ness
ness	ness	ment
ment	ment	ment

ment	ment	ment
ment	fully	fully
fully	fully	fully

2 2 2 2 2 2 2 2 2 2 2 2 2 2 2 2 2 2 2 2 2 2 2 2 2 2 2 2 2
2 2 2 2 2 2 2 2 2 2 2 2 2 2 2 2 2 2 2 2 2 2 2 2 2 2 2 2 2
2 2 2 2 2 2 2 2 2 2 2 2 2 2 2 2 2 2 2 2 2 2 2 2 2 2 2 2 2
2 2 2 2 2 2 2 2 2 2 2 2 2 2 2 2 2 2 2 2 2 2 2 2 2 2 2 2 2
2 2 2 2 2 2 2 2 2 2 2 2 2 2 2 2 2 2 2 2 2 2 2 2 2 2 2 2 2
2 2 2 2 2 2 2 2 2 2 2 2 2 2 2 2 2 2 2 2 2 2 2 2 2 2 2 2 2
2 2 2 2 2 2 2 2 2 2 2 2 2 2 2 2 2 2 2 2 2 2 2 2 2 2 2 2 2
2 2 2 2 2 2 2 2 2 2 2 2 2 2 2 2 2 2 2 2 2 2 2 2 2 2 2 2 2
2 2 2 2 2 2 2 2 2 2 2 2 2 2 2 2 2 2 2 2 2 2 2 2 2 2 2 2 2
2 2 2 2 2 2 2 2 2 2 2 2 2 2 2 2 2 2 2 2 2 2 2 2 2 2 2 2 2
2 2 2 2 2 2 2 2 2 2 2 2 2 2 2 2 2 2 2 2 2 2 2 2 2 2 2 2 2
2 2 2 2 2 2 2 2 2 2 2 2 2 2 2 2 2 2 2 2 2 2 2 2 2 2 2 2 2
2 2 2 2 2 2 2 2 2 2 2 2 2 2 2 2 2 2 2 2 2 2 2 2 2 2 2 2 2
2 2 2 2 2 2 2 2 2 2 2 2 2 2 2 2 2 2 2 2 2 2 2 2 2 2 2 2 2
2 2 2 2 2 2 2 2 2 2 2 2 2 2 2 2 2 2 2 2 2 2 2 2 2 2 2 2 2
2 2 2 2 2 2 2 2 2 2 2 2 2 2 2 2 2 2 2 2 2 2 2 2 2 2 2 2 2
2 2 2 2 2 2 2 2 2 2 2 2 2 2 2 2 2 2 2 2 2 2 2 2 2 2 2 2 2
2 2 2 2 2 2 2 2 2 2 2 2 2 2 2 2 2 2 2 2 2 2 2 2 2 2 2 2 2
2 2 2 2 2 2 2 2 2 2 2 2 2 2 2 2 2 2 2 2 2 2 2 2 2 2 2 2 2
2 2 2 2 2 2 2 2 2 2 2 2 2 2 2 2 2 2 2 2 2 2 2 2 2 2 2 2 2
2 2 2 2 2 2 2 2 2 2 2 2 2 2 2 2 2 2 2 2 2 2 2 2 2 2 2 2 2
2 2 2 2 2 2 2 2 2 2 2 2 2 2 2 2 2 2 2 2 2 2 2 2 2 2 2 2 2
2 2 2 2 2 2 2 2 2 2 2 2 2 2 2 2 2 2 2 2 2 2 2 2 2 2 2 2 2
2 2 2 2 2 2 2 2 2 2 2 2 2 2 2 2 2 2 2 2 2 2 2 2 2 2 2 2 2
2 2 2 2 2 2 2 2 2 2 2 2 2 2 2 2 2 2 2 2 2 2 2 2 2 2 2 2 2
2 2 2 2 2 2 2 2 2 2 2 2 2 2 2 2 2 2 2 2 2 2 2 2 2 2 2 2 2
2 2 2 2 2 2 2 2 2 2 2 2 2 2 2 2 2 2 2 2 2 2 2 2 2 2 2 2 2
2 2 2 2 2 2 2 2 2 2 2 2 2 2 2 2 2 2 2 2 2 2 2 2 2 2 2 2 2
2 2 2 2 2 2 2 2 2 2 2 2 2 2 2 2 2 2 2 2 2 2 2 2 2 2 2 2 2
2 2 2 2 2 2 2 2 2 2 2 2 2 2 2 2 2 2 2 2 2 2 2 2 2 2 2 2 2
2 2 2 2 2 2 2 2 2 2 2 2 2 2 2 2 2 2 2 2 2 2 2 2 2 2 2 2 2
2 2 2 2 2 2 2 2 2 2 2 2 2 2 2 2 2 2 2 2 2 2 2 2 2 2 2 2 2

fully	fully	fully
BONUS: your points x2	BONUS: your points x3	

2 2 2 2 2 2 2 2 2 2 2 2 2 2 2 2 2 2 2 2 2 2 2 2 2 2 2 2 2 2 2
2 2 2 2 2 2 2 2 2 2 2 2 2 2 2 2 2 2 2 2 2 2 2 2 2 2 2 2 2 2 2
2 2 2 2 2 2 2 2 2 2 2 2 2 2 2 2 2 2 2 2 2 2 2 2 2 2 2 2 2 2 2
2 2 2 2 2 2 2 2 2 2 2 2 2 2 2 2 2 2 2 2 2 2 2 2 2 2 2 2 2 2 2
2 2 2 2 2 2 2 2 2 2 2 2 2 2 2 2 2 2 2 2 2 2 2 2 2 2 2 2 2 2 2
2 2 2 2 2 2 2 2 2 2 2 2 2 2 2 2 2 2 2 2 2 2 2 2 2 2 2 2 2 2 2
2 2 2 2 2 2 2 2 2 2 2 2 2 2 2 2 2 2 2 2 2 2 2 2 2 2 2 2 2 2 2
2 2 2 2 2 2 2 2 2 2 2 2 2 2 2 2 2 2 2 2 2 2 2 2 2 2 2 2 2 2 2
2 2 2 2 2 2 2 2 2 2 2 2 2 2 2 2 2 2 2 2 2 2 2 2 2 2 2 2 2 2 2
2 2 2 2 2 2 2 2 2 2 2 2 2 2 2 2 2 2 2 2 2 2 2 2 2 2 2 2 2 2 2
2 2 2 2 2 2 2 2 2 2 2 2 2 2 2 2 2 2 2 2 2 2 2 2 2 2 2 2 2 2 2
2 2 2 2 2 2 2 2 2 2 2 2 2 2 2 2 2 2 2 2 2 2 2 2 2 2 2 2 2 2 2
2 2 2 2 2 2 2 2 2 2 2 2 2 2 2 2 2 2 2 2 2 2 2 2 2 2 2 2 2 2 2
2 2 2 2 2 2 2 2 2 2 2 2 2 2 2 2 2 2 2 2 2 2 2 2 2 2 2 2 2 2 2
2 2 2 2 2 2 2 2 2 2 2 2 2 2 2 2 2 2 2 2 2 2 2 2 2 2 2 2 2 2 2
2 2 2 2 2 2 2 2 2 2 2 2 2 2 2 2 2 2 2 2 2 2 2 2 2 2 2 2 2 2 2
2 2 2 2 2 2 2 2 2 2 2 2 2 2 2 2 2 2 2 2 2 2 2 2 2 2 2 2 2 2 2
2 2 2 2 2 2 2 2 2 2 2 2 2 2 2 2 2 2 2 2 2 2 2 2 2 2 2 2 2 2 2
2 2 2 2 2 2 2 2 2 2 2 2 2 2 2 2 2 2 2 2 2 2 2 2 2 2 2 2 2 2 2
2 2 2 2 2 2 2 2 2 2 2 2 2 2 2 2 2 2 2 2 2 2 2 2 2 2 2 2 2 2 2
2 2 2 2 2 2 2 2 2 2 2 2 2 2 2 2 2 2 2 2 2 2 2 2 2 2 2 2 2 2 2
2 2 2 2 2 2 2 2 2 2 2 2 2 2 2 2 2 2 2 2 2 2 2 2 2 2 2 2 2 2 2
2 2 2 2 2 2 2 2 2 2 2 2 2 2 2 2 2 2 2 2 2 2 2 2 2 2 2 2 2 2 2
2 2 2 2 2 2 2 2 2 2 2 2 2 2 2 2 2 2 2 2 2 2 2 2 2 2 2 2 2 2 2
2 2 2 2 2 2 2 2 2 2 2 2 2 2 2 2 2 2 2 2 2 2 2 2 2 2 2 2 2 2 2
2 2 2 2 2 2 2 2 2 2 2 2 2 2 2 2 2 2 2 2 2 2 2 2 2 2 2 2 2 2 2
2 2 2 2 2 2 2 2 2 2 2 2 2 2 2 2 2 2 2 2 2 2 2 2 2 2 2 2 2 2 2
2 2 2 2 2 2 2 2 2 2 2 2 2 2 2 2 2 2 2 2 2 2 2 2 2 2 2 2 2 2 2
2 2 2 2 2 2 2 2 2 2 2 2 2 2 2 2 2 2 2 2 2 2 2 2 2 2 2 2 2 2 2
2 2 2 2 2 2 2 2 2 2 2 2 2 2 2 2 2 2 2 2 2 2 2 2 2 2 2 2 2 2 2
2 2 2 2 2 2 2 2 2 2 2 2 2 2 2 2 2 2 2 2 2 2 2 2 2 2 2 2 2 2 2
2 2 2 2 2 2 2 2 2 2 2 2 2 2 2 2 2 2 2 2 2 2 2 2 2 2 2 2 2 2 2
2 2 2 2 2 2 2 2 2 2 2 2 2 2 2 2 2 2 2 2 2 2 2 2 2 2 2 2 2 2 2

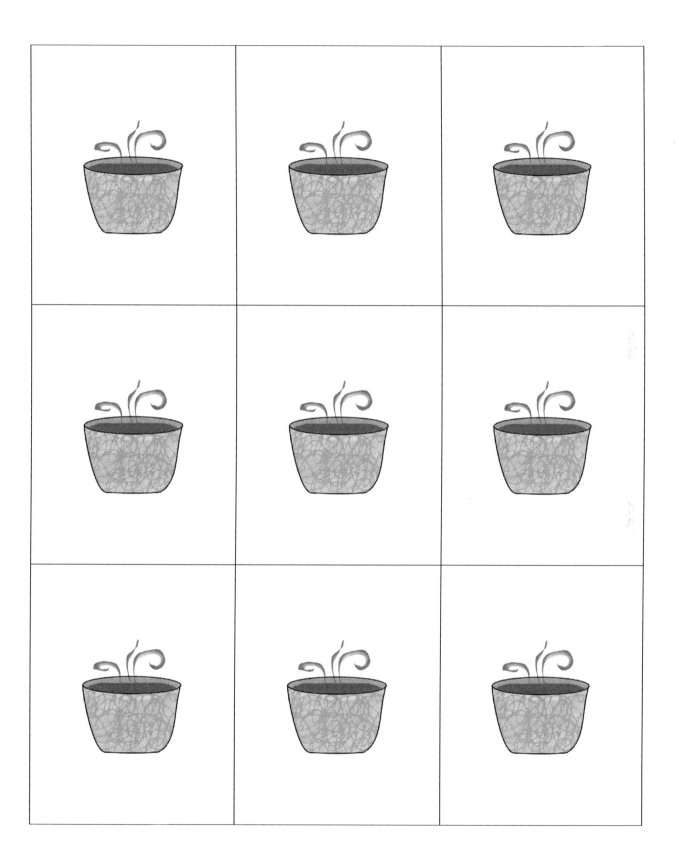

2 2 2 2 2 2 2 2 2 2 2 2 2 2 2 2 2 2 2 2 2 2 2 2 2 2 2 2 2 2
2 2 2 2 2 2 2 2 2 2 2 2 2 2 2 2 2 2 2 2 2 2 2 2 2 2 2 2 2 2
2 2 2 2 2 2 2 2 2 2 2 2 2 2 2 2 2 2 2 2 2 2 2 2 2 2 2 2 2 2
2 2 2 2 2 2 2 2 2 2 2 2 2 2 2 2 2 2 2 2 2 2 2 2 2 2 2 2 2 2
2 2 2 2 2 2 2 2 2 2 2 2 2 2 2 2 2 2 2 2 2 2 2 2 2 2 2 2 2 2
2 2 2 2 2 2 2 2 2 2 2 2 2 2 2 2 2 2 2 2 2 2 2 2 2 2 2 2 2 2
2 2 2 2 2 2 2 2 2 2 2 2 2 2 2 2 2 2 2 2 2 2 2 2 2 2 2 2 2 2
2 2 2 2 2 2 2 2 2 2 2 2 2 2 2 2 2 2 2 2 2 2 2 2 2 2 2 2 2 2
2 2 2 2 2 2 2 2 2 2 2 2 2 2 2 2 2 2 2 2 2 2 2 2 2 2 2 2 2 2
2 2 2 2 2 2 2 2 2 2 2 2 2 2 2 2 2 2 2 2 2 2 2 2 2 2 2 2 2 2
2 2 2 2 2 2 2 2 2 2 2 2 2 2 2 2 2 2 2 2 2 2 2 2 2 2 2 2 2 2
2 2 2 2 2 2 2 2 2 2 2 2 2 2 2 2 2 2 2 2 2 2 2 2 2 2 2 2 2 2
2 2 2 2 2 2 2 2 2 2 2 2 2 2 2 2 2 2 2 2 2 2 2 2 2 2 2 2 2 2
2 2 2 2 2 2 2 2 2 2 2 2 2 2 2 2 2 2 2 2 2 2 2 2 2 2 2 2 2 2
2 2 2 2 2 2 2 2 2 2 2 2 2 2 2 2 2 2 2 2 2 2 2 2 2 2 2 2 2 2
2 2 2 2 2 2 2 2 2 2 2 2 2 2 2 2 2 2 2 2 2 2 2 2 2 2 2 2 2 2
2 2 2 2 2 2 2 2 2 2 2 2 2 2 2 2 2 2 2 2 2 2 2 2 2 2 2 2 2 2
2 2 2 2 2 2 2 2 2 2 2 2 2 2 2 2 2 2 2 2 2 2 2 2 2 2 2 2 2 2
2 2 2 2 2 2 2 2 2 2 2 2 2 2 2 2 2 2 2 2 2 2 2 2 2 2 2 2 2 2
2 2 2 2 2 2 2 2 2 2 2 2 2 2 2 2 2 2 2 2 2 2 2 2 2 2 2 2 2 2
2 2 2 2 2 2 2 2 2 2 2 2 2 2 2 2 2 2 2 2 2 2 2 2 2 2 2 2 2 2
2 2 2 2 2 2 2 2 2 2 2 2 2 2 2 2 2 2 2 2 2 2 2 2 2 2 2 2 2 2
2 2 2 2 2 2 2 2 2 2 2 2 2 2 2 2 2 2 2 2 2 2 2 2 2 2 2 2 2 2
2 2 2 2 2 2 2 2 2 2 2 2 2 2 2 2 2 2 2 2 2 2 2 2 2 2 2 2 2 2
2 2 2 2 2 2 2 2 2 2 2 2 2 2 2 2 2 2 2 2 2 2 2 2 2 2 2 2 2 2
2 2 2 2 2 2 2 2 2 2 2 2 2 2 2 2 2 2 2 2 2 2 2 2 2 2 2 2 2 2
2 2 2 2 2 2 2 2 2 2 2 2 2 2 2 2 2 2 2 2 2 2 2 2 2 2 2 2 2 2
2 2 2 2 2 2 2 2 2 2 2 2 2 2 2 2 2 2 2 2 2 2 2 2 2 2 2 2 2 2
2 2 2 2 2 2 2 2 2 2 2 2 2 2 2 2 2 2 2 2 2 2 2 2 2 2 2 2 2 2
2 2 2 2 2 2 2 2 2 2 2 2 2 2 2 2 2 2 2 2 2 2 2 2 2 2 2 2 2 2
2 2 2 2 2 2 2 2 2 2 2 2 2 2 2 2 2 2 2 2 2 2 2 2 2 2 2 2 2 2
2 2 2 2 2 2 2 2 2 2 2 2 2 2 2 2 2 2 2 2 2 2 2 2 2 2 2 2 2 2
2 2 2 2 2 2 2 2 2 2 2 2 2 2 2 2 2 2 2 2 2 2 2 2 2 2 2 2 2 2
2 2 2 2 2 2 2 2 2 2 2 2 2 2 2 2 2 2 2 2 2 2 2 2 2 2 2 2 2 2
2 2 2 2 2 2 2 2 2 2 2 2 2 2 2 2 2 2 2 2 2 2 2 2 2 2 2 2 2 2

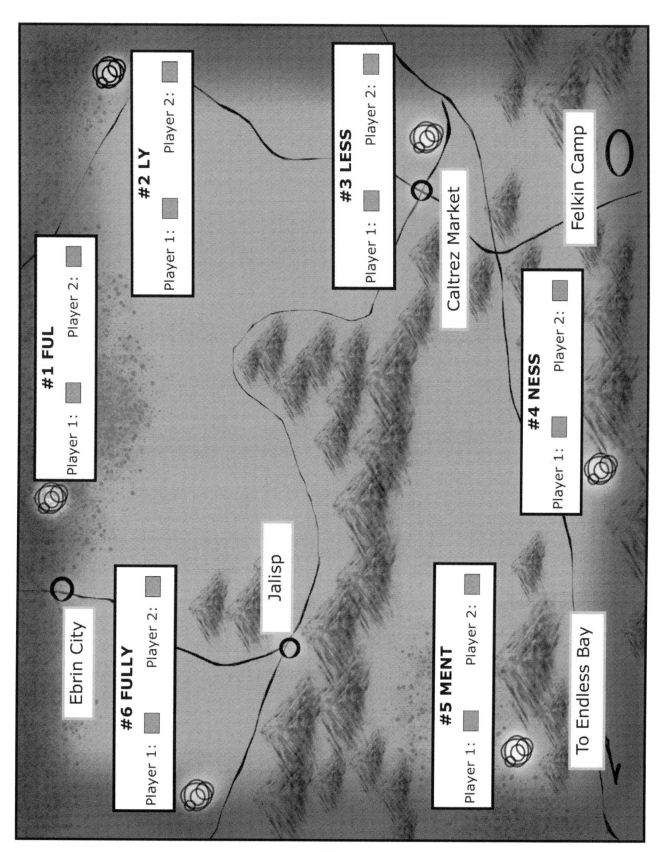

2 2 2 2 2 2 2 2 2 2 2 2 2 2 2 2 2 2 2 2 2 2 2 2 2 2 2 2 2 2 2 2 2 2
2 2 2 2 2 2 2 2 2 2 2 2 2 2 2 2 2 2 2 2 2 2 2 2 2 2 2 2 2 2 2 2 2 2
2 2 2 2 2 2 2 2 2 2 2 2 2 2 2 2 2 2 2 2 2 2 2 2 2 2 2 2 2 2 2 2 2 2
2 2 2 2 2 2 2 2 2 2 2 2 2 2 2 2 2 2 2 2 2 2 2 2 2 2 2 2 2 2 2 2 2 2
2 2 2 2 2 2 2 2 2 2 2 2 2 2 2 2 2 2 2 2 2 2 2 2 2 2 2 2 2 2 2 2 2 2
2 2 2 2 2 2 2 2 2 2 2 2 2 2 2 2 2 2 2 2 2 2 2 2 2 2 2 2 2 2 2 2 2 2
2 2 2 2 2 2 2 2 2 2 2 2 2 2 2 2 2 2 2 2 2 2 2 2 2 2 2 2 2 2 2 2 2 2
2 2 2 2 2 2 2 2 2 2 2 2 2 2 2 2 2 2 2 2 2 2 2 2 2 2 2 2 2 2 2 2 2 2
2 2 2 2 2 2 2 2 2 2 2 2 2 2 2 2 2 2 2 2 2 2 2 2 2 2 2 2 2 2 2 2 2 2
2 2 2 2 2 2 2 2 2 2 2 2 2 2 2 2 2 2 2 2 2 2 2 2 2 2 2 2 2 2 2 2 2 2
2 2 2 2 2 2 2 2 2 2 2 2 2 2 2 2 2 2 2 2 2 2 2 2 2 2 2 2 2 2 2 2 2 2
2 2 2 2 2 2 2 2 2 2 2 2 2 2 2 2 2 2 2 2 2 2 2 2 2 2 2 2 2 2 2 2 2 2
2 2 2 2 2 2 2 2 2 2 2 2 2 2 2 2 2 2 2 2 2 2 2 2 2 2 2 2 2 2 2 2 2 2
2 2 2 2 2 2 2 2 2 2 2 2 2 2 2 2 2 2 2 2 2 2 2 2 2 2 2 2 2 2 2 2 2 2
2 2 2 2 2 2 2 2 2 2 2 2 2 2 2 2 2 2 2 2 2 2 2 2 2 2 2 2 2 2 2 2 2 2
2 2 2 2 2 2 2 2 2 2 2 2 2 2 2 2 2 2 2 2 2 2 2 2 2 2 2 2 2 2 2 2 2 2
2 2 2 2 2 2 2 2 2 2 2 2 2 2 2 2 2 2 2 2 2 2 2 2 2 2 2 2 2 2 2 2 2 2
2 2 2 2 2 2 2 2 2 2 2 2 2 2 2 2 2 2 2 2 2 2 2 2 2 2 2 2 2 2 2 2 2 2
2 2 2 2 2 2 2 2 2 2 2 2 2 2 2 2 2 2 2 2 2 2 2 2 2 2 2 2 2 2 2 2 2 2
2 2 2 2 2 2 2 2 2 2 2 2 2 2 2 2 2 2 2 2 2 2 2 2 2 2 2 2 2 2 2 2 2 2
2 2 2 2 2 2 2 2 2 2 2 2 2 2 2 2 2 2 2 2 2 2 2 2 2 2 2 2 2 2 2 2 2 2
2 2 2 2 2 2 2 2 2 2 2 2 2 2 2 2 2 2 2 2 2 2 2 2 2 2 2 2 2 2 2 2 2 2
2 2 2 2 2 2 2 2 2 2 2 2 2 2 2 2 2 2 2 2 2 2 2 2 2 2 2 2 2 2 2 2 2 2
2 2 2 2 2 2 2 2 2 2 2 2 2 2 2 2 2 2 2 2 2 2 2 2 2 2 2 2 2 2 2 2 2 2
2 2 2 2 2 2 2 2 2 2 2 2 2 2 2 2 2 2 2 2 2 2 2 2 2 2 2 2 2 2 2 2 2 2
2 2 2 2 2 2 2 2 2 2 2 2 2 2 2 2 2 2 2 2 2 2 2 2 2 2 2 2 2 2 2 2 2 2
2 2 2 2 2 2 2 2 2 2 2 2 2 2 2 2 2 2 2 2 2 2 2 2 2 2 2 2 2 2 2 2 2 2
2 2 2 2 2 2 2 2 2 2 2 2 2 2 2 2 2 2 2 2 2 2 2 2 2 2 2 2 2 2 2 2 2 2
2 2 2 2 2 2 2 2 2 2 2 2 2 2 2 2 2 2 2 2 2 2 2 2 2 2 2 2 2 2 2 2 2 2
2 2 2 2 2 2 2 2 2 2 2 2 2 2 2 2 2 2 2 2 2 2 2 2 2 2 2 2 2 2 2 2 2 2
2 2 2 2 2 2 2 2 2 2 2 2 2 2 2 2 2 2 2 2 2 2 2 2 2 2 2 2 2 2 2 2 2 2
2 2 2 2 2 2 2 2 2 2 2 2 2 2 2 2 2 2 2 2 2 2 2 2 2 2 2 2 2 2 2 2 2 2
2 2 2 2 2 2 2 2 2 2 2 2 2 2 2 2 2 2 2 2 2 2 2 2 2 2 2 2 2 2 2 2 2 2
2 2 2 2 2 2 2 2 2 2 2 2 2 2 2 2 2 2 2 2 2 2 2 2 2 2 2 2 2 2 2 2 2 2
2 2 2 2 2 2 2 2 2 2 2 2 2 2 2 2 2 2 2 2 2 2 2 2 2 2 2 2 2 2 2 2 2 2

significantly	sadness	thoughtfully	endless
exactly	kindness	skillfully	helpless
quickly	exactness	successfully	painless
slowly	dryness	thankfully	thoughtless
boldly	freshness	regretfully	limitless

successful	ailment	recklessness counts for two
skillful	investment	aimlessly counts for two
helpful	enrichment	mindlessly counts for two
faithful	attachment	ruthlessly counts for two
eventful	containment	cheerfulness counts for two

2 2 2 2 2 2 2 2 2 2 2 2 2 2 2 2 2 2 2 2 2 2 2 2 2 2 2 2 2 2
2 2 2 2 2 2 2 2 2 2 2 2 2 2 2 2 2 2 2 2 2 2 2 2 2 2 2 2 2 2
2 2 2 2 2 2 2 2 2 2 2 2 2 2 2 2 2 2 2 2 2 2 2 2 2 2 2 2 2 2
2 2 2 2 2 2 2 2 2 2 2 2 2 2 2 2 2 2 2 2 2 2 2 2 2 2 2 2 2 2
2 2 2 2 2 2 2 2 2 2 2 2 2 2 2 2 2 2 2 2 2 2 2 2 2 2 2 2 2 2
2 2 2 2 2 2 2 2 2 2 2 2 2 2 2 2 2 2 2 2 2 2 2 2 2 2 2 2 2 2
2 2 2 2 2 2 2 2 2 2 2 2 2 2 2 2 2 2 2 2 2 2 2 2 2 2 2 2 2 2
2 2 2 2 2 2 2 2 2 2 2 2 2 2 2 2 2 2 2 2 2 2 2 2 2 2 2 2 2 2
2 2 2 2 2 2 2 2 2 2 2 2 2 2 2 2 2 2 2 2 2 2 2 2 2 2 2 2 2 2
2 2 2 2 2 2 2 2 2 2 2 2 2 2 2 2 2 2 2 2 2 2 2 2 2 2 2 2 2 2
2 2 2 2 2 2 2 2 2 2 2 2 2 2 2 2 2 2 2 2 2 2 2 2 2 2 2 2 2 2
2 2 2 2 2 2 2 2 2 2 2 2 2 2 2 2 2 2 2 2 2 2 2 2 2 2 2 2 2 2
2 2 2 2 2 2 2 2 2 2 2 2 2 2 2 2 2 2 2 2 2 2 2 2 2 2 2 2 2 2
2 2 2 2 2 2 2 2 2 2 2 2 2 2 2 2 2 2 2 2 2 2 2 2 2 2 2 2 2 2
2 2 2 2 2 2 2 2 2 2 2 2 2 2 2 2 2 2 2 2 2 2 2 2 2 2 2 2 2 2
2 2 2 2 2 2 2 2 2 2 2 2 2 2 2 2 2 2 2 2 2 2 2 2 2 2 2 2 2 2
2 2 2 2 2 2 2 2 2 2 2 2 2 2 2 2 2 2 2 2 2 2 2 2 2 2 2 2 2 2
2 2 2 2 2 2 2 2 2 2 2 2 2 2 2 2 2 2 2 2 2 2 2 2 2 2 2 2 2 2
2 2 2 2 2 2 2 2 2 2 2 2 2 2 2 2 2 2 2 2 2 2 2 2 2 2 2 2 2 2
2 2 2 2 2 2 2 2 2 2 2 2 2 2 2 2 2 2 2 2 2 2 2 2 2 2 2 2 2 2
2 2 2 2 2 2 2 2 2 2 2 2 2 2 2 2 2 2 2 2 2 2 2 2 2 2 2 2 2 2
2 2 2 2 2 2 2 2 2 2 2 2 2 2 2 2 2 2 2 2 2 2 2 2 2 2 2 2 2 2
2 2 2 2 2 2 2 2 2 2 2 2 2 2 2 2 2 2 2 2 2 2 2 2 2 2 2 2 2 2
2 2 2 2 2 2 2 2 2 2 2 2 2 2 2 2 2 2 2 2 2 2 2 2 2 2 2 2 2 2
2 2 2 2 2 2 2 2 2 2 2 2 2 2 2 2 2 2 2 2 2 2 2 2 2 2 2 2 2 2
2 2 2 2 2 2 2 2 2 2 2 2 2 2 2 2 2 2 2 2 2 2 2 2 2 2 2 2 2 2
2 2 2 2 2 2 2 2 2 2 2 2 2 2 2 2 2 2 2 2 2 2 2 2 2 2 2 2 2 2
2 2 2 2 2 2 2 2 2 2 2 2 2 2 2 2 2 2 2 2 2 2 2 2 2 2 2 2 2 2
2 2 2 2 2 2 2 2 2 2 2 2 2 2 2 2 2 2 2 2 2 2 2 2 2 2 2 2 2 2
2 2 2 2 2 2 2 2 2 2 2 2 2 2 2 2 2 2 2 2 2 2 2 2 2 2 2 2 2 2
2 2 2 2 2 2 2 2 2 2 2 2 2 2 2 2 2 2 2 2 2 2 2 2 2 2 2 2 2 2
2 2 2 2 2 2 2 2 2 2 2 2 2 2 2 2 2 2 2 2 2 2 2 2 2 2 2 2 2 2
2 2 2 2 2 2 2 2 2 2 2 2 2 2 2 2 2 2 2 2 2 2 2 2 2 2 2 2 2 2

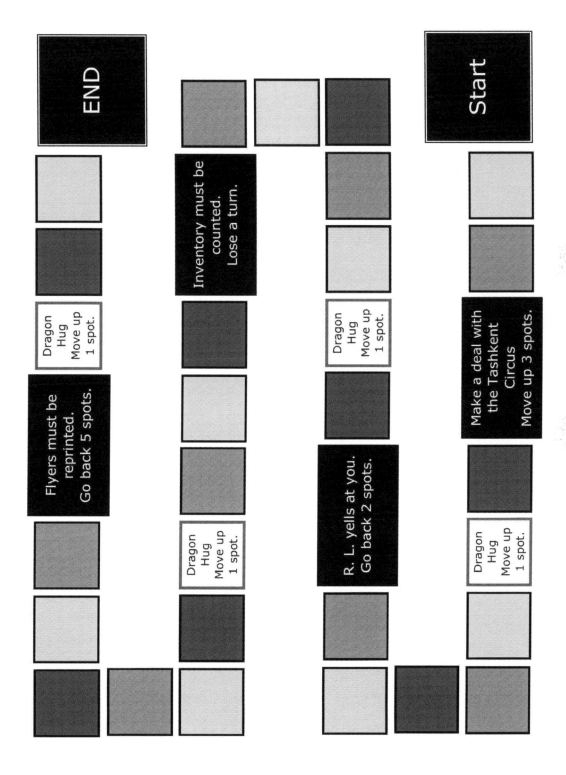

START

END

Make a deal with the Tashkent Circus
Move up 3 spots.

Dragon Hug
Move up 1 spot.

R. L. yells at you.
Go back 2 spots.

Dragon Hug
Move up 1 spot.

Inventory must be counted.
Lose a turn.

Dragon Hug
Move up 1 spot.

Flyers must be reprinted.
Go back 5 spots.

Dragon Hug
Move up 1 spot.

3 3 3 3 3 3 3 3 3 3 3 3 3 3 3 3 3 3 3 3 3 3 3 3 3 3 3 3 3 3 3 3 3 3 3 3
3 3 3 3 3 3 3 3 3 3 3 3 3 3 3 3 3 3 3 3 3 3 3 3 3 3 3 3 3 3 3 3 3 3 3 3
3 3 3 3 3 3 3 3 3 3 3 3 3 3 3 3 3 3 3 3 3 3 3 3 3 3 3 3 3 3 3 3 3 3 3 3
3 3 3 3 3 3 3 3 3 3 3 3 3 3 3 3 3 3 3 3 3 3 3 3 3 3 3 3 3 3 3 3 3 3 3 3
3 3 3 3 3 3 3 3 3 3 3 3 3 3 3 3 3 3 3 3 3 3 3 3 3 3 3 3 3 3 3 3 3 3 3 3
3 3 3 3 3 3 3 3 3 3 3 3 3 3 3 3 3 3 3 3 3 3 3 3 3 3 3 3 3 3 3 3 3 3 3 3
3 3 3 3 3 3 3 3 3 3 3 3 3 3 3 3 3 3 3 3 3 3 3 3 3 3 3 3 3 3 3 3 3 3 3 3
3 3 3 3 3 3 3 3 3 3 3 3 3 3 3 3 3 3 3 3 3 3 3 3 3 3 3 3 3 3 3 3 3 3 3 3
3 3 3 3 3 3 3 3 3 3 3 3 3 3 3 3 3 3 3 3 3 3 3 3 3 3 3 3 3 3 3 3 3 3 3 3
3 3 3 3 3 3 3 3 3 3 3 3 3 3 3 3 3 3 3 3 3 3 3 3 3 3 3 3 3 3 3 3 3 3 3 3
3 3 3 3 3 3 3 3 3 3 3 3 3 3 3 3 3 3 3 3 3 3 3 3 3 3 3 3 3 3 3 3 3 3 3 3
3 3 3 3 3 3 3 3 3 3 3 3 3 3 3 3 3 3 3 3 3 3 3 3 3 3 3 3 3 3 3 3 3 3 3 3
3 3 3 3 3 3 3 3 3 3 3 3 3 3 3 3 3 3 3 3 3 3 3 3 3 3 3 3 3 3 3 3 3 3 3 3
3 3 3 3 3 3 3 3 3 3 3 3 3 3 3 3 3 3 3 3 3 3 3 3 3 3 3 3 3 3 3 3 3 3 3 3
3 3 3 3 3 3 3 3 3 3 3 3 3 3 3 3 3 3 3 3 3 3 3 3 3 3 3 3 3 3 3 3 3 3 3 3
3 3 3 3 3 3 3 3 3 3 3 3 3 3 3 3 3 3 3 3 3 3 3 3 3 3 3 3 3 3 3 3 3 3 3 3
3 3 3 3 3 3 3 3 3 3 3 3 3 3 3 3 3 3 3 3 3 3 3 3 3 3 3 3 3 3 3 3 3 3 3 3
3 3 3 3 3 3 3 3 3 3 3 3 3 3 3 3 3 3 3 3 3 3 3 3 3 3 3 3 3 3 3 3 3 3 3 3
3 3 3 3 3 3 3 3 3 3 3 3 3 3 3 3 3 3 3 3 3 3 3 3 3 3 3 3 3 3 3 3 3 3 3 3
3 3 3 3 3 3 3 3 3 3 3 3 3 3 3 3 3 3 3 3 3 3 3 3 3 3 3 3 3 3 3 3 3 3 3 3
3 3 3 3 3 3 3 3 3 3 3 3 3 3 3 3 3 3 3 3 3 3 3 3 3 3 3 3 3 3 3 3 3 3 3 3
3 3 3 3 3 3 3 3 3 3 3 3 3 3 3 3 3 3 3 3 3 3 3 3 3 3 3 3 3 3 3 3 3 3 3 3
3 3 3 3 3 3 3 3 3 3 3 3 3 3 3 3 3 3 3 3 3 3 3 3 3 3 3 3 3 3 3 3 3 3 3 3
3 3 3 3 3 3 3 3 3 3 3 3 3 3 3 3 3 3 3 3 3 3 3 3 3 3 3 3 3 3 3 3 3 3 3 3
3 3 3 3 3 3 3 3 3 3 3 3 3 3 3 3 3 3 3 3 3 3 3 3 3 3 3 3 3 3 3 3 3 3 3 3
3 3 3 3 3 3 3 3 3 3 3 3 3 3 3 3 3 3 3 3 3 3 3 3 3 3 3 3 3 3 3 3 3 3 3 3
3 3 3 3 3 3 3 3 3 3 3 3 3 3 3 3 3 3 3 3 3 3 3 3 3 3 3 3 3 3 3 3 3 3 3 3
3 3 3 3 3 3 3 3 3 3 3 3 3 3 3 3 3 3 3 3 3 3 3 3 3 3 3 3 3 3 3 3 3 3 3 3
3 3 3 3 3 3 3 3 3 3 3 3 3 3 3 3 3 3 3 3 3 3 3 3 3 3 3 3 3 3 3 3 3 3 3 3
3 3 3 3 3 3 3 3 3 3 3 3 3 3 3 3 3 3 3 3 3 3 3 3 3 3 3 3 3 3 3 3 3 3 3 3
3 3 3 3 3 3 3 3 3 3 3 3 3 3 3 3 3 3 3 3 3 3 3 3 3 3 3 3 3 3 3 3 3 3 3 3
3 3 3 3 3 3 3 3 3 3 3 3 3 3 3 3 3 3 3 3 3 3 3 3 3 3 3 3 3 3 3 3 3 3 3 3

planning	finishing	feeding	setting
shredding	nodded	training	aggravated
playing	beginning	omitted	getting
jotted	passing	trotted	popping
letting	sitting	trimming	planted

3 3 3 3 3 3 3 3 3 3 3 3 3 3 3 3 3 3 3 3 3 3 3 3 3 3 3 3 3 3 3 3 3
3 3 3 3 3 3 3 3 3 3 3 3 3 3 3 3 3 3 3 3 3 3 3 3 3 3 3 3 3 3 3 3 3
3 3 3 3 3 3 3 3 3 3 3 3 3 3 3 3 3 3 3 3 3 3 3 3 3 3 3 3 3 3 3 3 3
3 3 3 3 3 3 3 3 3 3 3 3 3 3 3 3 3 3 3 3 3 3 3 3 3 3 3 3 3 3 3 3 3
3 3 3 3 3 3 3 3 3 3 3 3 3 3 3 3 3 3 3 3 3 3 3 3 3 3 3 3 3 3 3 3 3
3 3 3 3 3 3 3 3 3 3 3 3 3 3 3 3 3 3 3 3 3 3 3 3 3 3 3 3 3 3 3 3 3
3 3 3 3 3 3 3 3 3 3 3 3 3 3 3 3 3 3 3 3 3 3 3 3 3 3 3 3 3 3 3 3 3
3 3 3 3 3 3 3 3 3 3 3 3 3 3 3 3 3 3 3 3 3 3 3 3 3 3 3 3 3 3 3 3 3
3 3 3 3 3 3 3 3 3 3 3 3 3 3 3 3 3 3 3 3 3 3 3 3 3 3 3 3 3 3 3 3 3
3 3 3 3 3 3 3 3 3 3 3 3 3 3 3 3 3 3 3 3 3 3 3 3 3 3 3 3 3 3 3 3 3
3 3 3 3 3 3 3 3 3 3 3 3 3 3 3 3 3 3 3 3 3 3 3 3 3 3 3 3 3 3 3 3 3
3 3 3 3 3 3 3 3 3 3 3 3 3 3 3 3 3 3 3 3 3 3 3 3 3 3 3 3 3 3 3 3 3
3 3 3 3 3 3 3 3 3 3 3 3 3 3 3 3 3 3 3 3 3 3 3 3 3 3 3 3 3 3 3 3 3
3 3 3 3 3 3 3 3 3 3 3 3 3 3 3 3 3 3 3 3 3 3 3 3 3 3 3 3 3 3 3 3 3
3 3 3 3 3 3 3 3 3 3 3 3 3 3 3 3 3 3 3 3 3 3 3 3 3 3 3 3 3 3 3 3 3
3 3 3 3 3 3 3 3 3 3 3 3 3 3 3 3 3 3 3 3 3 3 3 3 3 3 3 3 3 3 3 3 3
3 3 3 3 3 3 3 3 3 3 3 3 3 3 3 3 3 3 3 3 3 3 3 3 3 3 3 3 3 3 3 3 3
3 3 3 3 3 3 3 3 3 3 3 3 3 3 3 3 3 3 3 3 3 3 3 3 3 3 3 3 3 3 3 3 3
3 3 3 3 3 3 3 3 3 3 3 3 3 3 3 3 3 3 3 3 3 3 3 3 3 3 3 3 3 3 3 3 3
3 3 3 3 3 3 3 3 3 3 3 3 3 3 3 3 3 3 3 3 3 3 3 3 3 3 3 3 3 3 3 3 3
3 3 3 3 3 3 3 3 3 3 3 3 3 3 3 3 3 3 3 3 3 3 3 3 3 3 3 3 3 3 3 3 3
3 3 3 3 3 3 3 3 3 3 3 3 3 3 3 3 3 3 3 3 3 3 3 3 3 3 3 3 3 3 3 3 3
3 3 3 3 3 3 3 3 3 3 3 3 3 3 3 3 3 3 3 3 3 3 3 3 3 3 3 3 3 3 3 3 3
3 3 3 3 3 3 3 3 3 3 3 3 3 3 3 3 3 3 3 3 3 3 3 3 3 3 3 3 3 3 3 3 3
3 3 3 3 3 3 3 3 3 3 3 3 3 3 3 3 3 3 3 3 3 3 3 3 3 3 3 3 3 3 3 3 3
3 3 3 3 3 3 3 3 3 3 3 3 3 3 3 3 3 3 3 3 3 3 3 3 3 3 3 3 3 3 3 3 3
3 3 3 3 3 3 3 3 3 3 3 3 3 3 3 3 3 3 3 3 3 3 3 3 3 3 3 3 3 3 3 3 3
3 3 3 3 3 3 3 3 3 3 3 3 3 3 3 3 3 3 3 3 3 3 3 3 3 3 3 3 3 3 3 3 3
3 3 3 3 3 3 3 3 3 3 3 3 3 3 3 3 3 3 3 3 3 3 3 3 3 3 3 3 3 3 3 3 3
3 3 3 3 3 3 3 3 3 3 3 3 3 3 3 3 3 3 3 3 3 3 3 3 3 3 3 3 3 3 3 3 3
3 3 3 3 3 3 3 3 3 3 3 3 3 3 3 3 3 3 3 3 3 3 3 3 3 3 3 3 3 3 3 3 3
3 3 3 3 3 3 3 3 3 3 3 3 3 3 3 3 3 3 3 3 3 3 3 3 3 3 3 3 3 3 3 3 3

packing	hopping	dropping	dripping
shredded	nodding	planting	rubbing
batted	batting	shopping	running
asking	saying	chatting	chatted
omitting	trotting	jotting	sifted

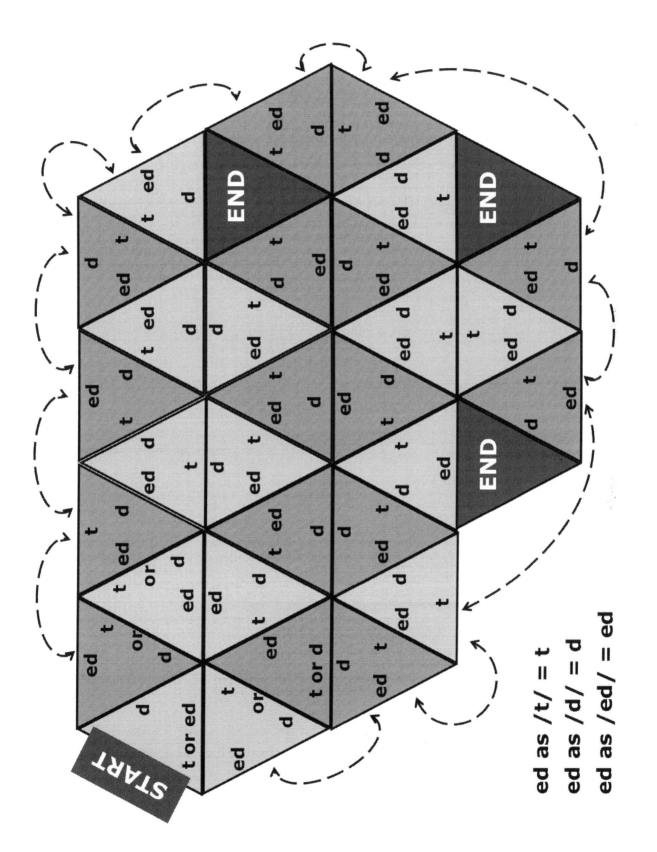

ed as /t/ = t

ed as /d/ = d

ed as /ed/ = ed

4 4 4 4 4 4 4 4 4 4 4 4 4 4 4 4 4 4 4 4 4 4 4 4 4 4 4 4 4 4 4 4 4 4
4 4 4 4 4 4 4 4 4 4 4 4 4 4 4 4 4 4 4 4 4 4 4 4 4 4 4 4 4 4 4 4 4 4
4 4 4 4 4 4 4 4 4 4 4 4 4 4 4 4 4 4 4 4 4 4 4 4 4 4 4 4 4 4 4 4 4 4
4 4 4 4 4 4 4 4 4 4 4 4 4 4 4 4 4 4 4 4 4 4 4 4 4 4 4 4 4 4 4 4 4 4
4 4 4 4 4 4 4 4 4 4 4 4 4 4 4 4 4 4 4 4 4 4 4 4 4 4 4 4 4 4 4 4 4 4
4 4 4 4 4 4 4 4 4 4 4 4 4 4 4 4 4 4 4 4 4 4 4 4 4 4 4 4 4 4 4 4 4 4
4 4 4 4 4 4 4 4 4 4 4 4 4 4 4 4 4 4 4 4 4 4 4 4 4 4 4 4 4 4 4 4 4 4
4 4 4 4 4 4 4 4 4 4 4 4 4 4 4 4 4 4 4 4 4 4 4 4 4 4 4 4 4 4 4 4 4 4
4 4 4 4 4 4 4 4 4 4 4 4 4 4 4 4 4 4 4 4 4 4 4 4 4 4 4 4 4 4 4 4 4 4
4 4 4 4 4 4 4 4 4 4 4 4 4 4 4 4 4 4 4 4 4 4 4 4 4 4 4 4 4 4 4 4 4 4
4 4 4 4 4 4 4 4 4 4 4 4 4 4 4 4 4 4 4 4 4 4 4 4 4 4 4 4 4 4 4 4 4 4
4 4 4 4 4 4 4 4 4 4 4 4 4 4 4 4 4 4 4 4 4 4 4 4 4 4 4 4 4 4 4 4 4 4
4 4 4 4 4 4 4 4 4 4 4 4 4 4 4 4 4 4 4 4 4 4 4 4 4 4 4 4 4 4 4 4 4 4
4 4 4 4 4 4 4 4 4 4 4 4 4 4 4 4 4 4 4 4 4 4 4 4 4 4 4 4 4 4 4 4 4 4
4 4 4 4 4 4 4 4 4 4 4 4 4 4 4 4 4 4 4 4 4 4 4 4 4 4 4 4 4 4 4 4 4 4
4 4 4 4 4 4 4 4 4 4 4 4 4 4 4 4 4 4 4 4 4 4 4 4 4 4 4 4 4 4 4 4 4 4
4 4 4 4 4 4 4 4 4 4 4 4 4 4 4 4 4 4 4 4 4 4 4 4 4 4 4 4 4 4 4 4 4 4
4 4 4 4 4 4 4 4 4 4 4 4 4 4 4 4 4 4 4 4 4 4 4 4 4 4 4 4 4 4 4 4 4 4
4 4 4 4 4 4 4 4 4 4 4 4 4 4 4 4 4 4 4 4 4 4 4 4 4 4 4 4 4 4 4 4 4 4
4 4 4 4 4 4 4 4 4 4 4 4 4 4 4 4 4 4 4 4 4 4 4 4 4 4 4 4 4 4 4 4 4 4
4 4 4 4 4 4 4 4 4 4 4 4 4 4 4 4 4 4 4 4 4 4 4 4 4 4 4 4 4 4 4 4 4 4
4 4 4 4 4 4 4 4 4 4 4 4 4 4 4 4 4 4 4 4 4 4 4 4 4 4 4 4 4 4 4 4 4 4
4 4 4 4 4 4 4 4 4 4 4 4 4 4 4 4 4 4 4 4 4 4 4 4 4 4 4 4 4 4 4 4 4 4
4 4 4 4 4 4 4 4 4 4 4 4 4 4 4 4 4 4 4 4 4 4 4 4 4 4 4 4 4 4 4 4 4 4
4 4 4 4 4 4 4 4 4 4 4 4 4 4 4 4 4 4 4 4 4 4 4 4 4 4 4 4 4 4 4 4 4 4
4 4 4 4 4 4 4 4 4 4 4 4 4 4 4 4 4 4 4 4 4 4 4 4 4 4 4 4 4 4 4 4 4 4
4 4 4 4 4 4 4 4 4 4 4 4 4 4 4 4 4 4 4 4 4 4 4 4 4 4 4 4 4 4 4 4 4 4
4 4 4 4 4 4 4 4 4 4 4 4 4 4 4 4 4 4 4 4 4 4 4 4 4 4 4 4 4 4 4 4 4 4
4 4 4 4 4 4 4 4 4 4 4 4 4 4 4 4 4 4 4 4 4 4 4 4 4 4 4 4 4 4 4 4 4 4
4 4 4 4 4 4 4 4 4 4 4 4 4 4 4 4 4 4 4 4 4 4 4 4 4 4 4 4 4 4 4 4 4 4
4 4 4 4 4 4 4 4 4 4 4 4 4 4 4 4 4 4 4 4 4 4 4 4 4 4 4 4 4 4 4 4 4 4
4 4 4 4 4 4 4 4 4 4 4 4 4 4 4 4 4 4 4 4 4 4 4 4 4 4 4 4 4 4 4 4 4 4
4 4 4 4 4 4 4 4 4 4 4 4 4 4 4 4 4 4 4 4 4 4 4 4 4 4 4 4 4 4 4 4 4 4

answered	finished	misted	completed
added	helped	wanted	nodded
traveled	thanked	minded	spotted
thrilled	hopped	responded	lasted
skilled	hoped	kidded	rusted

exclaimed	looked	sprayed	inched
happened	skipped	robbed	locked
followed	backed	sailed	mixed
delayed	snacked	trimmed	boxed
spilled	gripped	grilled	shocked

		trapper
container	deeper	wildest
optimist	difficulty	fallen

5 5 5 5 5 5 5 5 5 5 5 5 5 5 5 5 5 5 5 5 5 5 5 5 5 5 5 5 5 5
5 5 5 5 5 5 5 5 5 5 5 5 5 5 5 5 5 5 5 5 5 5 5 5 5 5 5 5 5 5
5 5 5 5 5 5 5 5 5 5 5 5 5 5 5 5 5 5 5 5 5 5 5 5 5 5 5 5 5 5
5 5 5 5 5 5 5 5 5 5 5 5 5 5 5 5 5 5 5 5 5 5 5 5 5 5 5 5 5 5
5 5 5 5 5 5 5 5 5 5 5 5 5 5 5 5 5 5 5 5 5 5 5 5 5 5 5 5 5 5
5 5 5 5 5 5 5 5 5 5 5 5 5 5 5 5 5 5 5 5 5 5 5 5 5 5 5 5 5 5
5 5 5 5 5 5 5 5 5 5 5 5 5 5 5 5 5 5 5 5 5 5 5 5 5 5 5 5 5 5
5 5 5 5 5 5 5 5 5 5 5 5 5 5 5 5 5 5 5 5 5 5 5 5 5 5 5 5 5 5
5 5 5 5 5 5 5 5 5 5 5 5 5 5 5 5 5 5 5 5 5 5 5 5 5 5 5 5 5 5
5 5 5 5 5 5 5 5 5 5 5 5 5 5 5 5 5 5 5 5 5 5 5 5 5 5 5 5 5 5
5 5 5 5 5 5 5 5 5 5 5 5 5 5 5 5 5 5 5 5 5 5 5 5 5 5 5 5 5 5
5 5 5 5 5 5 5 5 5 5 5 5 5 5 5 5 5 5 5 5 5 5 5 5 5 5 5 5 5 5
5 5 5 5 5 5 5 5 5 5 5 5 5 5 5 5 5 5 5 5 5 5 5 5 5 5 5 5 5 5
5 5 5 5 5 5 5 5 5 5 5 5 5 5 5 5 5 5 5 5 5 5 5 5 5 5 5 5 5 5
5 5 5 5 5 5 5 5 5 5 5 5 5 5 5 5 5 5 5 5 5 5 5 5 5 5 5 5 5 5
5 5 5 5 5 5 5 5 5 5 5 5 5 5 5 5 5 5 5 5 5 5 5 5 5 5 5 5 5 5
5 5 5 5 5 5 5 5 5 5 5 5 5 5 5 5 5 5 5 5 5 5 5 5 5 5 5 5 5 5
5 5 5 5 5 5 5 5 5 5 5 5 5 5 5 5 5 5 5 5 5 5 5 5 5 5 5 5 5 5
5 5 5 5 5 5 5 5 5 5 5 5 5 5 5 5 5 5 5 5 5 5 5 5 5 5 5 5 5 5
5 5 5 5 5 5 5 5 5 5 5 5 5 5 5 5 5 5 5 5 5 5 5 5 5 5 5 5 5 5
5 5 5 5 5 5 5 5 5 5 5 5 5 5 5 5 5 5 5 5 5 5 5 5 5 5 5 5 5 5
5 5 5 5 5 5 5 5 5 5 5 5 5 5 5 5 5 5 5 5 5 5 5 5 5 5 5 5 5 5
5 5 5 5 5 5 5 5 5 5 5 5 5 5 5 5 5 5 5 5 5 5 5 5 5 5 5 5 5 5
5 5 5 5 5 5 5 5 5 5 5 5 5 5 5 5 5 5 5 5 5 5 5 5 5 5 5 5 5 5
5 5 5 5 5 5 5 5 5 5 5 5 5 5 5 5 5 5 5 5 5 5 5 5 5 5 5 5 5 5
5 5 5 5 5 5 5 5 5 5 5 5 5 5 5 5 5 5 5 5 5 5 5 5 5 5 5 5 5 5
5 5 5 5 5 5 5 5 5 5 5 5 5 5 5 5 5 5 5 5 5 5 5 5 5 5 5 5 5 5
5 5 5 5 5 5 5 5 5 5 5 5 5 5 5 5 5 5 5 5 5 5 5 5 5 5 5 5 5 5
5 5 5 5 5 5 5 5 5 5 5 5 5 5 5 5 5 5 5 5 5 5 5 5 5 5 5 5 5 5
5 5 5 5 5 5 5 5 5 5 5 5 5 5 5 5 5 5 5 5 5 5 5 5 5 5 5 5 5 5
5 5 5 5 5 5 5 5 5 5 5 5 5 5 5 5 5 5 5 5 5 5 5 5 5 5 5 5 5 5
5 5 5 5 5 5 5 5 5 5 5 5 5 5 5 5 5 5 5 5 5 5 5 5 5 5 5 5 5 5
5 5 5 5 5 5 5 5 5 5 5 5 5 5 5 5 5 5 5 5 5 5 5 5 5 5 5 5 5 5
5 5 5 5 5 5 5 5 5 5 5 5 5 5 5 5 5 5 5 5 5 5 5 5 5 5 5 5 5 5

outlandish	predictable	complexity
fisher	toaster	faster
bravest	soloist	gritty

5 5 5 5 5 5 5 5 5 5 5 5 5 5 5 5 5 5 5 5 5 5 5 5 5 5 5 5 5 5 5 5
5 5 5 5 5 5 5 5 5 5 5 5 5 5 5 5 5 5 5 5 5 5 5 5 5 5 5 5 5 5 5 5
5 5 5 5 5 5 5 5 5 5 5 5 5 5 5 5 5 5 5 5 5 5 5 5 5 5 5 5 5 5 5 5
5 5 5 5 5 5 5 5 5 5 5 5 5 5 5 5 5 5 5 5 5 5 5 5 5 5 5 5 5 5 5 5
5 5 5 5 5 5 5 5 5 5 5 5 5 5 5 5 5 5 5 5 5 5 5 5 5 5 5 5 5 5 5 5
5 5 5 5 5 5 5 5 5 5 5 5 5 5 5 5 5 5 5 5 5 5 5 5 5 5 5 5 5 5 5 5
5 5 5 5 5 5 5 5 5 5 5 5 5 5 5 5 5 5 5 5 5 5 5 5 5 5 5 5 5 5 5 5
5 5 5 5 5 5 5 5 5 5 5 5 5 5 5 5 5 5 5 5 5 5 5 5 5 5 5 5 5 5 5 5
5 5 5 5 5 5 5 5 5 5 5 5 5 5 5 5 5 5 5 5 5 5 5 5 5 5 5 5 5 5 5 5
5 5 5 5 5 5 5 5 5 5 5 5 5 5 5 5 5 5 5 5 5 5 5 5 5 5 5 5 5 5 5 5
5 5 5 5 5 5 5 5 5 5 5 5 5 5 5 5 5 5 5 5 5 5 5 5 5 5 5 5 5 5 5 5
5 5 5 5 5 5 5 5 5 5 5 5 5 5 5 5 5 5 5 5 5 5 5 5 5 5 5 5 5 5 5 5
5 5 5 5 5 5 5 5 5 5 5 5 5 5 5 5 5 5 5 5 5 5 5 5 5 5 5 5 5 5 5 5
5 5 5 5 5 5 5 5 5 5 5 5 5 5 5 5 5 5 5 5 5 5 5 5 5 5 5 5 5 5 5 5
5 5 5 5 5 5 5 5 5 5 5 5 5 5 5 5 5 5 5 5 5 5 5 5 5 5 5 5 5 5 5 5
5 5 5 5 5 5 5 5 5 5 5 5 5 5 5 5 5 5 5 5 5 5 5 5 5 5 5 5 5 5 5 5
5 5 5 5 5 5 5 5 5 5 5 5 5 5 5 5 5 5 5 5 5 5 5 5 5 5 5 5 5 5 5 5
5 5 5 5 5 5 5 5 5 5 5 5 5 5 5 5 5 5 5 5 5 5 5 5 5 5 5 5 5 5 5 5
5 5 5 5 5 5 5 5 5 5 5 5 5 5 5 5 5 5 5 5 5 5 5 5 5 5 5 5 5 5 5 5
5 5 5 5 5 5 5 5 5 5 5 5 5 5 5 5 5 5 5 5 5 5 5 5 5 5 5 5 5 5 5 5
5 5 5 5 5 5 5 5 5 5 5 5 5 5 5 5 5 5 5 5 5 5 5 5 5 5 5 5 5 5 5 5
5 5 5 5 5 5 5 5 5 5 5 5 5 5 5 5 5 5 5 5 5 5 5 5 5 5 5 5 5 5 5 5
5 5 5 5 5 5 5 5 5 5 5 5 5 5 5 5 5 5 5 5 5 5 5 5 5 5 5 5 5 5 5 5
5 5 5 5 5 5 5 5 5 5 5 5 5 5 5 5 5 5 5 5 5 5 5 5 5 5 5 5 5 5 5 5
5 5 5 5 5 5 5 5 5 5 5 5 5 5 5 5 5 5 5 5 5 5 5 5 5 5 5 5 5 5 5 5
5 5 5 5 5 5 5 5 5 5 5 5 5 5 5 5 5 5 5 5 5 5 5 5 5 5 5 5 5 5 5 5
5 5 5 5 5 5 5 5 5 5 5 5 5 5 5 5 5 5 5 5 5 5 5 5 5 5 5 5 5 5 5 5
5 5 5 5 5 5 5 5 5 5 5 5 5 5 5 5 5 5 5 5 5 5 5 5 5 5 5 5 5 5 5 5
5 5 5 5 5 5 5 5 5 5 5 5 5 5 5 5 5 5 5 5 5 5 5 5 5 5 5 5 5 5 5 5
5 5 5 5 5 5 5 5 5 5 5 5 5 5 5 5 5 5 5 5 5 5 5 5 5 5 5 5 5 5 5 5
5 5 5 5 5 5 5 5 5 5 5 5 5 5 5 5 5 5 5 5 5 5 5 5 5 5 5 5 5 5 5 5
5 5 5 5 5 5 5 5 5 5 5 5 5 5 5 5 5 5 5 5 5 5 5 5 5 5 5 5 5 5 5 5
5 5 5 5 5 5 5 5 5 5 5 5 5 5 5 5 5 5 5 5 5 5 5 5 5 5 5 5 5 5 5 5
5 5 5 5 5 5 5 5 5 5 5 5 5 5 5 5 5 5 5 5 5 5 5 5 5 5 5 5 5 5 5 5

hidden	unselfish	attainable
possibility		

5 5 5 5 5 5 5 5 5 5 5 5 5 5 5 5 5 5 5 5 5 5 5 5 5 5 5 5 5 5
5 5 5 5 5 5 5 5 5 5 5 5 5 5 5 5 5 5 5 5 5 5 5 5 5 5 5 5 5 5
5 5 5 5 5 5 5 5 5 5 5 5 5 5 5 5 5 5 5 5 5 5 5 5 5 5 5 5 5 5
5 5 5 5 5 5 5 5 5 5 5 5 5 5 5 5 5 5 5 5 5 5 5 5 5 5 5 5 5 5
5 5 5 5 5 5 5 5 5 5 5 5 5 5 5 5 5 5 5 5 5 5 5 5 5 5 5 5 5 5
5 5 5 5 5 5 5 5 5 5 5 5 5 5 5 5 5 5 5 5 5 5 5 5 5 5 5 5 5 5
5 5 5 5 5 5 5 5 5 5 5 5 5 5 5 5 5 5 5 5 5 5 5 5 5 5 5 5 5 5
5 5 5 5 5 5 5 5 5 5 5 5 5 5 5 5 5 5 5 5 5 5 5 5 5 5 5 5 5 5
5 5 5 5 5 5 5 5 5 5 5 5 5 5 5 5 5 5 5 5 5 5 5 5 5 5 5 5 5 5
5 5 5 5 5 5 5 5 5 5 5 5 5 5 5 5 5 5 5 5 5 5 5 5 5 5 5 5 5 5
5 5 5 5 5 5 5 5 5 5 5 5 5 5 5 5 5 5 5 5 5 5 5 5 5 5 5 5 5 5
5 5 5 5 5 5 5 5 5 5 5 5 5 5 5 5 5 5 5 5 5 5 5 5 5 5 5 5 5 5
5 5 5 5 5 5 5 5 5 5 5 5 5 5 5 5 5 5 5 5 5 5 5 5 5 5 5 5 5 5
5 5 5 5 5 5 5 5 5 5 5 5 5 5 5 5 5 5 5 5 5 5 5 5 5 5 5 5 5 5
5 5 5 5 5 5 5 5 5 5 5 5 5 5 5 5 5 5 5 5 5 5 5 5 5 5 5 5 5 5
5 5 5 5 5 5 5 5 5 5 5 5 5 5 5 5 5 5 5 5 5 5 5 5 5 5 5 5 5 5
5 5 5 5 5 5 5 5 5 5 5 5 5 5 5 5 5 5 5 5 5 5 5 5 5 5 5 5 5 5
5 5 5 5 5 5 5 5 5 5 5 5 5 5 5 5 5 5 5 5 5 5 5 5 5 5 5 5 5 5
5 5 5 5 5 5 5 5 5 5 5 5 5 5 5 5 5 5 5 5 5 5 5 5 5 5 5 5 5 5
5 5 5 5 5 5 5 5 5 5 5 5 5 5 5 5 5 5 5 5 5 5 5 5 5 5 5 5 5 5
5 5 5 5 5 5 5 5 5 5 5 5 5 5 5 5 5 5 5 5 5 5 5 5 5 5 5 5 5 5
5 5 5 5 5 5 5 5 5 5 5 5 5 5 5 5 5 5 5 5 5 5 5 5 5 5 5 5 5 5
5 5 5 5 5 5 5 5 5 5 5 5 5 5 5 5 5 5 5 5 5 5 5 5 5 5 5 5 5 5
5 5 5 5 5 5 5 5 5 5 5 5 5 5 5 5 5 5 5 5 5 5 5 5 5 5 5 5 5 5
5 5 5 5 5 5 5 5 5 5 5 5 5 5 5 5 5 5 5 5 5 5 5 5 5 5 5 5 5 5
5 5 5 5 5 5 5 5 5 5 5 5 5 5 5 5 5 5 5 5 5 5 5 5 5 5 5 5 5 5
5 5 5 5 5 5 5 5 5 5 5 5 5 5 5 5 5 5 5 5 5 5 5 5 5 5 5 5 5 5
5 5 5 5 5 5 5 5 5 5 5 5 5 5 5 5 5 5 5 5 5 5 5 5 5 5 5 5 5 5
5 5 5 5 5 5 5 5 5 5 5 5 5 5 5 5 5 5 5 5 5 5 5 5 5 5 5 5 5 5
5 5 5 5 5 5 5 5 5 5 5 5 5 5 5 5 5 5 5 5 5 5 5 5 5 5 5 5 5 5
5 5 5 5 5 5 5 5 5 5 5 5 5 5 5 5 5 5 5 5 5 5 5 5 5 5 5 5 5 5
5 5 5 5 5 5 5 5 5 5 5 5 5 5 5 5 5 5 5 5 5 5 5 5 5 5 5 5 5 5

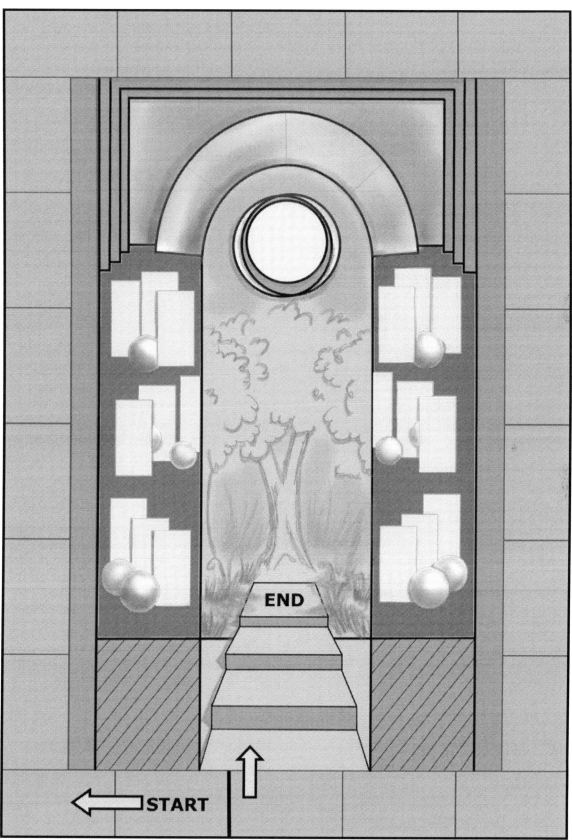

END

START

6 6 6 6 6 6 6 6 6 6 6 6 6 6 6 6 6 6 6 6 6 6 6 6 6 6 6 6 6 6 6
6 6 6 6 6 6 6 6 6 6 6 6 6 6 6 6 6 6 6 6 6 6 6 6 6 6 6 6 6 6 6
6 6 6 6 6 6 6 6 6 6 6 6 6 6 6 6 6 6 6 6 6 6 6 6 6 6 6 6 6 6 6
6 6 6 6 6 6 6 6 6 6 6 6 6 6 6 6 6 6 6 6 6 6 6 6 6 6 6 6 6 6 6
6 6 6 6 6 6 6 6 6 6 6 6 6 6 6 6 6 6 6 6 6 6 6 6 6 6 6 6 6 6 6
6 6 6 6 6 6 6 6 6 6 6 6 6 6 6 6 6 6 6 6 6 6 6 6 6 6 6 6 6 6 6
6 6 6 6 6 6 6 6 6 6 6 6 6 6 6 6 6 6 6 6 6 6 6 6 6 6 6 6 6 6 6
6 6 6 6 6 6 6 6 6 6 6 6 6 6 6 6 6 6 6 6 6 6 6 6 6 6 6 6 6 6 6
6 6 6 6 6 6 6 6 6 6 6 6 6 6 6 6 6 6 6 6 6 6 6 6 6 6 6 6 6 6 6
6 6 6 6 6 6 6 6 6 6 6 6 6 6 6 6 6 6 6 6 6 6 6 6 6 6 6 6 6 6 6
6 6 6 6 6 6 6 6 6 6 6 6 6 6 6 6 6 6 6 6 6 6 6 6 6 6 6 6 6 6 6
6 6 6 6 6 6 6 6 6 6 6 6 6 6 6 6 6 6 6 6 6 6 6 6 6 6 6 6 6 6 6
6 6 6 6 6 6 6 6 6 6 6 6 6 6 6 6 6 6 6 6 6 6 6 6 6 6 6 6 6 6 6
6 6 6 6 6 6 6 6 6 6 6 6 6 6 6 6 6 6 6 6 6 6 6 6 6 6 6 6 6 6 6
6 6 6 6 6 6 6 6 6 6 6 6 6 6 6 6 6 6 6 6 6 6 6 6 6 6 6 6 6 6 6
6 6 6 6 6 6 6 6 6 6 6 6 6 6 6 6 6 6 6 6 6 6 6 6 6 6 6 6 6 6 6
6 6 6 6 6 6 6 6 6 6 6 6 6 6 6 6 6 6 6 6 6 6 6 6 6 6 6 6 6 6 6
6 6 6 6 6 6 6 6 6 6 6 6 6 6 6 6 6 6 6 6 6 6 6 6 6 6 6 6 6 6 6
6 6 6 6 6 6 6 6 6 6 6 6 6 6 6 6 6 6 6 6 6 6 6 6 6 6 6 6 6 6 6
6 6 6 6 6 6 6 6 6 6 6 6 6 6 6 6 6 6 6 6 6 6 6 6 6 6 6 6 6 6 6
6 6 6 6 6 6 6 6 6 6 6 6 6 6 6 6 6 6 6 6 6 6 6 6 6 6 6 6 6 6 6
6 6 6 6 6 6 6 6 6 6 6 6 6 6 6 6 6 6 6 6 6 6 6 6 6 6 6 6 6 6 6
6 6 6 6 6 6 6 6 6 6 6 6 6 6 6 6 6 6 6 6 6 6 6 6 6 6 6 6 6 6 6
6 6 6 6 6 6 6 6 6 6 6 6 6 6 6 6 6 6 6 6 6 6 6 6 6 6 6 6 6 6 6
6 6 6 6 6 6 6 6 6 6 6 6 6 6 6 6 6 6 6 6 6 6 6 6 6 6 6 6 6 6 6
6 6 6 6 6 6 6 6 6 6 6 6 6 6 6 6 6 6 6 6 6 6 6 6 6 6 6 6 6 6 6
6 6 6 6 6 6 6 6 6 6 6 6 6 6 6 6 6 6 6 6 6 6 6 6 6 6 6 6 6 6 6
6 6 6 6 6 6 6 6 6 6 6 6 6 6 6 6 6 6 6 6 6 6 6 6 6 6 6 6 6 6 6
6 6 6 6 6 6 6 6 6 6 6 6 6 6 6 6 6 6 6 6 6 6 6 6 6 6 6 6 6 6 6
6 6 6 6 6 6 6 6 6 6 6 6 6 6 6 6 6 6 6 6 6 6 6 6 6 6 6 6 6 6 6
6 6 6 6 6 6 6 6 6 6 6 6 6 6 6 6 6 6 6 6 6 6 6 6 6 6 6 6 6 6 6
6 6 6 6 6 6 6 6 6 6 6 6 6 6 6 6 6 6 6 6 6 6 6 6 6 6 6 6 6 6 6
6 6 6 6 6 6 6 6 6 6 6 6 6 6 6 6 6 6 6 6 6 6 6 6 6 6 6 6 6 6 6
6 6 6 6 6 6 6 6 6 6 6 6 6 6 6 6 6 6 6 6 6 6 6 6 6 6 6 6 6 6 6

try tried trying	yucky yuckier	gutsy gutsier gutsiest
envy envying enviable	rely reliable relying	nasty nastier nastiest
spy spying spied spies	empty emptying emptier emptiest	silky silkier silkiness
sickly sickliest	copy copier copying	play playful
dry drier drying	plenty plentiful	duty dutiful

6 6 6 6 6 6 6 6 6 6 6 6 6 6 6 6 6 6 6 6 6 6 6 6 6 6 6 6 6 6 6 6
6 6 6 6 6 6 6 6 6 6 6 6 6 6 6 6 6 6 6 6 6 6 6 6 6 6 6 6 6 6 6 6
6 6 6 6 6 6 6 6 6 6 6 6 6 6 6 6 6 6 6 6 6 6 6 6 6 6 6 6 6 6 6 6
6 6 6 6 6 6 6 6 6 6 6 6 6 6 6 6 6 6 6 6 6 6 6 6 6 6 6 6 6 6 6 6
6 6 6 6 6 6 6 6 6 6 6 6 6 6 6 6 6 6 6 6 6 6 6 6 6 6 6 6 6 6 6 6
6 6 6 6 6 6 6 6 6 6 6 6 6 6 6 6 6 6 6 6 6 6 6 6 6 6 6 6 6 6 6 6
6 6 6 6 6 6 6 6 6 6 6 6 6 6 6 6 6 6 6 6 6 6 6 6 6 6 6 6 6 6 6 6
6 6 6 6 6 6 6 6 6 6 6 6 6 6 6 6 6 6 6 6 6 6 6 6 6 6 6 6 6 6 6 6
6 6 6 6 6 6 6 6 6 6 6 6 6 6 6 6 6 6 6 6 6 6 6 6 6 6 6 6 6 6 6 6
6 6 6 6 6 6 6 6 6 6 6 6 6 6 6 6 6 6 6 6 6 6 6 6 6 6 6 6 6 6 6 6
6 6 6 6 6 6 6 6 6 6 6 6 6 6 6 6 6 6 6 6 6 6 6 6 6 6 6 6 6 6 6 6
6 6 6 6 6 6 6 6 6 6 6 6 6 6 6 6 6 6 6 6 6 6 6 6 6 6 6 6 6 6 6 6
6 6 6 6 6 6 6 6 6 6 6 6 6 6 6 6 6 6 6 6 6 6 6 6 6 6 6 6 6 6 6 6
6 6 6 6 6 6 6 6 6 6 6 6 6 6 6 6 6 6 6 6 6 6 6 6 6 6 6 6 6 6 6 6
6 6 6 6 6 6 6 6 6 6 6 6 6 6 6 6 6 6 6 6 6 6 6 6 6 6 6 6 6 6 6 6
6 6 6 6 6 6 6 6 6 6 6 6 6 6 6 6 6 6 6 6 6 6 6 6 6 6 6 6 6 6 6 6
6 6 6 6 6 6 6 6 6 6 6 6 6 6 6 6 6 6 6 6 6 6 6 6 6 6 6 6 6 6 6 6
6 6 6 6 6 6 6 6 6 6 6 6 6 6 6 6 6 6 6 6 6 6 6 6 6 6 6 6 6 6 6 6
6 6 6 6 6 6 6 6 6 6 6 6 6 6 6 6 6 6 6 6 6 6 6 6 6 6 6 6 6 6 6 6
6 6 6 6 6 6 6 6 6 6 6 6 6 6 6 6 6 6 6 6 6 6 6 6 6 6 6 6 6 6 6 6
6 6 6 6 6 6 6 6 6 6 6 6 6 6 6 6 6 6 6 6 6 6 6 6 6 6 6 6 6 6 6 6
6 6 6 6 6 6 6 6 6 6 6 6 6 6 6 6 6 6 6 6 6 6 6 6 6 6 6 6 6 6 6 6
6 6 6 6 6 6 6 6 6 6 6 6 6 6 6 6 6 6 6 6 6 6 6 6 6 6 6 6 6 6 6 6
6 6 6 6 6 6 6 6 6 6 6 6 6 6 6 6 6 6 6 6 6 6 6 6 6 6 6 6 6 6 6 6
6 6 6 6 6 6 6 6 6 6 6 6 6 6 6 6 6 6 6 6 6 6 6 6 6 6 6 6 6 6 6 6
6 6 6 6 6 6 6 6 6 6 6 6 6 6 6 6 6 6 6 6 6 6 6 6 6 6 6 6 6 6 6 6
6 6 6 6 6 6 6 6 6 6 6 6 6 6 6 6 6 6 6 6 6 6 6 6 6 6 6 6 6 6 6 6
6 6 6 6 6 6 6 6 6 6 6 6 6 6 6 6 6 6 6 6 6 6 6 6 6 6 6 6 6 6 6 6
6 6 6 6 6 6 6 6 6 6 6 6 6 6 6 6 6 6 6 6 6 6 6 6 6 6 6 6 6 6 6 6
6 6 6 6 6 6 6 6 6 6 6 6 6 6 6 6 6 6 6 6 6 6 6 6 6 6 6 6 6 6 6 6
6 6 6 6 6 6 6 6 6 6 6 6 6 6 6 6 6 6 6 6 6 6 6 6 6 6 6 6 6 6 6 6
6 6 6 6 6 6 6 6 6 6 6 6 6 6 6 6 6 6 6 6 6 6 6 6 6 6 6 6 6 6 6 6

baby babied babying babies	snowy snowier snowiest	display displaying displayed
justify justified justifying justifiable	say saying says	fly flying flies
soapy soapier	cry crying crier cried	lowly lowliest
smelly smellier smelliest	qualify qualified qualifies qualifiable	mushy mushier mushiest
chewy chewiness	funny funnier funniness	sway swaying sways

6 6 6 6 6 6 6 6 6 6 6 6 6 6 6 6 6 6 6 6 6 6 6 6 6 6 6 6 6 6
6 6 6 6 6 6 6 6 6 6 6 6 6 6 6 6 6 6 6 6 6 6 6 6 6 6 6 6 6 6
6 6 6 6 6 6 6 6 6 6 6 6 6 6 6 6 6 6 6 6 6 6 6 6 6 6 6 6 6 6
6 6 6 6 6 6 6 6 6 6 6 6 6 6 6 6 6 6 6 6 6 6 6 6 6 6 6 6 6 6
6 6 6 6 6 6 6 6 6 6 6 6 6 6 6 6 6 6 6 6 6 6 6 6 6 6 6 6 6 6
6 6 6 6 6 6 6 6 6 6 6 6 6 6 6 6 6 6 6 6 6 6 6 6 6 6 6 6 6 6
6 6 6 6 6 6 6 6 6 6 6 6 6 6 6 6 6 6 6 6 6 6 6 6 6 6 6 6 6 6
6 6 6 6 6 6 6 6 6 6 6 6 6 6 6 6 6 6 6 6 6 6 6 6 6 6 6 6 6 6
6 6 6 6 6 6 6 6 6 6 6 6 6 6 6 6 6 6 6 6 6 6 6 6 6 6 6 6 6 6
6 6 6 6 6 6 6 6 6 6 6 6 6 6 6 6 6 6 6 6 6 6 6 6 6 6 6 6 6 6
6 6 6 6 6 6 6 6 6 6 6 6 6 6 6 6 6 6 6 6 6 6 6 6 6 6 6 6 6 6
6 6 6 6 6 6 6 6 6 6 6 6 6 6 6 6 6 6 6 6 6 6 6 6 6 6 6 6 6 6
6 6 6 6 6 6 6 6 6 6 6 6 6 6 6 6 6 6 6 6 6 6 6 6 6 6 6 6 6 6
6 6 6 6 6 6 6 6 6 6 6 6 6 6 6 6 6 6 6 6 6 6 6 6 6 6 6 6 6 6
6 6 6 6 6 6 6 6 6 6 6 6 6 6 6 6 6 6 6 6 6 6 6 6 6 6 6 6 6 6
6 6 6 6 6 6 6 6 6 6 6 6 6 6 6 6 6 6 6 6 6 6 6 6 6 6 6 6 6 6
6 6 6 6 6 6 6 6 6 6 6 6 6 6 6 6 6 6 6 6 6 6 6 6 6 6 6 6 6 6
6 6 6 6 6 6 6 6 6 6 6 6 6 6 6 6 6 6 6 6 6 6 6 6 6 6 6 6 6 6
6 6 6 6 6 6 6 6 6 6 6 6 6 6 6 6 6 6 6 6 6 6 6 6 6 6 6 6 6 6
6 6 6 6 6 6 6 6 6 6 6 6 6 6 6 6 6 6 6 6 6 6 6 6 6 6 6 6 6 6
6 6 6 6 6 6 6 6 6 6 6 6 6 6 6 6 6 6 6 6 6 6 6 6 6 6 6 6 6 6
6 6 6 6 6 6 6 6 6 6 6 6 6 6 6 6 6 6 6 6 6 6 6 6 6 6 6 6 6 6
6 6 6 6 6 6 6 6 6 6 6 6 6 6 6 6 6 6 6 6 6 6 6 6 6 6 6 6 6 6
6 6 6 6 6 6 6 6 6 6 6 6 6 6 6 6 6 6 6 6 6 6 6 6 6 6 6 6 6 6
6 6 6 6 6 6 6 6 6 6 6 6 6 6 6 6 6 6 6 6 6 6 6 6 6 6 6 6 6 6
6 6 6 6 6 6 6 6 6 6 6 6 6 6 6 6 6 6 6 6 6 6 6 6 6 6 6 6 6 6
6 6 6 6 6 6 6 6 6 6 6 6 6 6 6 6 6 6 6 6 6 6 6 6 6 6 6 6 6 6
6 6 6 6 6 6 6 6 6 6 6 6 6 6 6 6 6 6 6 6 6 6 6 6 6 6 6 6 6 6
6 6 6 6 6 6 6 6 6 6 6 6 6 6 6 6 6 6 6 6 6 6 6 6 6 6 6 6 6 6
6 6 6 6 6 6 6 6 6 6 6 6 6 6 6 6 6 6 6 6 6 6 6 6 6 6 6 6 6 6
6 6 6 6 6 6 6 6 6 6 6 6 6 6 6 6 6 6 6 6 6 6 6 6 6 6 6 6 6 6
6 6 6 6 6 6 6 6 6 6 6 6 6 6 6 6 6 6 6 6 6 6 6 6 6 6 6 6 6 6
6 6 6 6 6 6 6 6 6 6 6 6 6 6 6 6 6 6 6 6 6 6 6 6 6 6 6 6 6 6
6 6 6 6 6 6 6 6 6 6 6 6 6 6 6 6 6 6 6 6 6 6 6 6 6 6 6 6 6 6

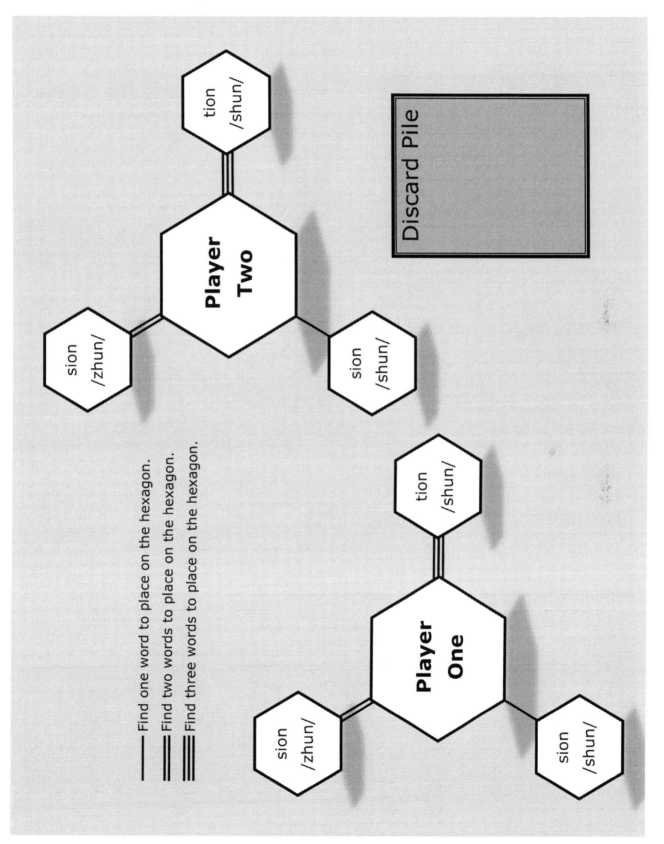

Discard Pile

Player Two

tion /shun/

sion /zhun/

sion /shun/

Player One

tion /shun/

sion /zhun/

sion /shun/

— Find one word to place on the hexagon.
═ Find two words to place on the hexagon.
≡ Find three words to place on the hexagon.

7 7 7 7 7 7 7 7 7 7 7 7 7 7 7 7 7 7 7 7 7 7 7 7 7 7 7 7 7 7 7
7 7 7 7 7 7 7 7 7 7 7 7 7 7 7 7 7 7 7 7 7 7 7 7 7 7 7 7 7 7 7
7 7 7 7 7 7 7 7 7 7 7 7 7 7 7 7 7 7 7 7 7 7 7 7 7 7 7 7 7 7 7
7 7 7 7 7 7 7 7 7 7 7 7 7 7 7 7 7 7 7 7 7 7 7 7 7 7 7 7 7 7 7
7 7 7 7 7 7 7 7 7 7 7 7 7 7 7 7 7 7 7 7 7 7 7 7 7 7 7 7 7 7 7
7 7 7 7 7 7 7 7 7 7 7 7 7 7 7 7 7 7 7 7 7 7 7 7 7 7 7 7 7 7 7
7 7 7 7 7 7 7 7 7 7 7 7 7 7 7 7 7 7 7 7 7 7 7 7 7 7 7 7 7 7 7
7 7 7 7 7 7 7 7 7 7 7 7 7 7 7 7 7 7 7 7 7 7 7 7 7 7 7 7 7 7 7
7 7 7 7 7 7 7 7 7 7 7 7 7 7 7 7 7 7 7 7 7 7 7 7 7 7 7 7 7 7 7
7 7 7 7 7 7 7 7 7 7 7 7 7 7 7 7 7 7 7 7 7 7 7 7 7 7 7 7 7 7 7
7 7 7 7 7 7 7 7 7 7 7 7 7 7 7 7 7 7 7 7 7 7 7 7 7 7 7 7 7 7 7
7 7 7 7 7 7 7 7 7 7 7 7 7 7 7 7 7 7 7 7 7 7 7 7 7 7 7 7 7 7 7
7 7 7 7 7 7 7 7 7 7 7 7 7 7 7 7 7 7 7 7 7 7 7 7 7 7 7 7 7 7 7
7 7 7 7 7 7 7 7 7 7 7 7 7 7 7 7 7 7 7 7 7 7 7 7 7 7 7 7 7 7 7
7 7 7 7 7 7 7 7 7 7 7 7 7 7 7 7 7 7 7 7 7 7 7 7 7 7 7 7 7 7 7
7 7 7 7 7 7 7 7 7 7 7 7 7 7 7 7 7 7 7 7 7 7 7 7 7 7 7 7 7 7 7
7 7 7 7 7 7 7 7 7 7 7 7 7 7 7 7 7 7 7 7 7 7 7 7 7 7 7 7 7 7 7
7 7 7 7 7 7 7 7 7 7 7 7 7 7 7 7 7 7 7 7 7 7 7 7 7 7 7 7 7 7 7
7 7 7 7 7 7 7 7 7 7 7 7 7 7 7 7 7 7 7 7 7 7 7 7 7 7 7 7 7 7 7
7 7 7 7 7 7 7 7 7 7 7 7 7 7 7 7 7 7 7 7 7 7 7 7 7 7 7 7 7 7 7
7 7 7 7 7 7 7 7 7 7 7 7 7 7 7 7 7 7 7 7 7 7 7 7 7 7 7 7 7 7 7
7 7 7 7 7 7 7 7 7 7 7 7 7 7 7 7 7 7 7 7 7 7 7 7 7 7 7 7 7 7 7
7 7 7 7 7 7 7 7 7 7 7 7 7 7 7 7 7 7 7 7 7 7 7 7 7 7 7 7 7 7 7
7 7 7 7 7 7 7 7 7 7 7 7 7 7 7 7 7 7 7 7 7 7 7 7 7 7 7 7 7 7 7
7 7 7 7 7 7 7 7 7 7 7 7 7 7 7 7 7 7 7 7 7 7 7 7 7 7 7 7 7 7 7
7 7 7 7 7 7 7 7 7 7 7 7 7 7 7 7 7 7 7 7 7 7 7 7 7 7 7 7 7 7 7
7 7 7 7 7 7 7 7 7 7 7 7 7 7 7 7 7 7 7 7 7 7 7 7 7 7 7 7 7 7 7
7 7 7 7 7 7 7 7 7 7 7 7 7 7 7 7 7 7 7 7 7 7 7 7 7 7 7 7 7 7 7
7 7 7 7 7 7 7 7 7 7 7 7 7 7 7 7 7 7 7 7 7 7 7 7 7 7 7 7 7 7 7
7 7 7 7 7 7 7 7 7 7 7 7 7 7 7 7 7 7 7 7 7 7 7 7 7 7 7 7 7 7 7
7 7 7 7 7 7 7 7 7 7 7 7 7 7 7 7 7 7 7 7 7 7 7 7 7 7 7 7 7 7 7
7 7 7 7 7 7 7 7 7 7 7 7 7 7 7 7 7 7 7 7 7 7 7 7 7 7 7 7 7 7 7

reputation	confusion	compassion
accommodation	cohesion	compulsion
solution	collision	mission
injection	television	impression
fraction	fusion	emulsion

attention	explosion	extension
direction	revision	rejection
potion	illusion	option
motion	occasion	vacation
location	precision	section

7 7 7 7 7 7 7 7 7 7 7 7 7 7 7 7 7 7 7 7 7 7 7 7 7 7 7 7 7 7 7 7 7 7 7
7 7 7 7 7 7 7 7 7 7 7 7 7 7 7 7 7 7 7 7 7 7 7 7 7 7 7 7 7 7 7 7 7 7 7
7 7 7 7 7 7 7 7 7 7 7 7 7 7 7 7 7 7 7 7 7 7 7 7 7 7 7 7 7 7 7 7 7 7 7
7 7 7 7 7 7 7 7 7 7 7 7 7 7 7 7 7 7 7 7 7 7 7 7 7 7 7 7 7 7 7 7 7 7 7
7 7 7 7 7 7 7 7 7 7 7 7 7 7 7 7 7 7 7 7 7 7 7 7 7 7 7 7 7 7 7 7 7 7 7
7 7 7 7 7 7 7 7 7 7 7 7 7 7 7 7 7 7 7 7 7 7 7 7 7 7 7 7 7 7 7 7 7 7 7
7 7 7 7 7 7 7 7 7 7 7 7 7 7 7 7 7 7 7 7 7 7 7 7 7 7 7 7 7 7 7 7 7 7 7
7 7 7 7 7 7 7 7 7 7 7 7 7 7 7 7 7 7 7 7 7 7 7 7 7 7 7 7 7 7 7 7 7 7 7
7 7 7 7 7 7 7 7 7 7 7 7 7 7 7 7 7 7 7 7 7 7 7 7 7 7 7 7 7 7 7 7 7 7 7
7 7 7 7 7 7 7 7 7 7 7 7 7 7 7 7 7 7 7 7 7 7 7 7 7 7 7 7 7 7 7 7 7 7 7
7 7 7 7 7 7 7 7 7 7 7 7 7 7 7 7 7 7 7 7 7 7 7 7 7 7 7 7 7 7 7 7 7 7 7
7 7 7 7 7 7 7 7 7 7 7 7 7 7 7 7 7 7 7 7 7 7 7 7 7 7 7 7 7 7 7 7 7 7 7
7 7 7 7 7 7 7 7 7 7 7 7 7 7 7 7 7 7 7 7 7 7 7 7 7 7 7 7 7 7 7 7 7 7 7
7 7 7 7 7 7 7 7 7 7 7 7 7 7 7 7 7 7 7 7 7 7 7 7 7 7 7 7 7 7 7 7 7 7 7
7 7 7 7 7 7 7 7 7 7 7 7 7 7 7 7 7 7 7 7 7 7 7 7 7 7 7 7 7 7 7 7 7 7 7
7 7 7 7 7 7 7 7 7 7 7 7 7 7 7 7 7 7 7 7 7 7 7 7 7 7 7 7 7 7 7 7 7 7 7
7 7 7 7 7 7 7 7 7 7 7 7 7 7 7 7 7 7 7 7 7 7 7 7 7 7 7 7 7 7 7 7 7 7 7
7 7 7 7 7 7 7 7 7 7 7 7 7 7 7 7 7 7 7 7 7 7 7 7 7 7 7 7 7 7 7 7 7 7 7
7 7 7 7 7 7 7 7 7 7 7 7 7 7 7 7 7 7 7 7 7 7 7 7 7 7 7 7 7 7 7 7 7 7 7
7 7 7 7 7 7 7 7 7 7 7 7 7 7 7 7 7 7 7 7 7 7 7 7 7 7 7 7 7 7 7 7 7 7 7
7 7 7 7 7 7 7 7 7 7 7 7 7 7 7 7 7 7 7 7 7 7 7 7 7 7 7 7 7 7 7 7 7 7 7
7 7 7 7 7 7 7 7 7 7 7 7 7 7 7 7 7 7 7 7 7 7 7 7 7 7 7 7 7 7 7 7 7 7 7
7 7 7 7 7 7 7 7 7 7 7 7 7 7 7 7 7 7 7 7 7 7 7 7 7 7 7 7 7 7 7 7 7 7 7
7 7 7 7 7 7 7 7 7 7 7 7 7 7 7 7 7 7 7 7 7 7 7 7 7 7 7 7 7 7 7 7 7 7 7
7 7 7 7 7 7 7 7 7 7 7 7 7 7 7 7 7 7 7 7 7 7 7 7 7 7 7 7 7 7 7 7 7 7 7
7 7 7 7 7 7 7 7 7 7 7 7 7 7 7 7 7 7 7 7 7 7 7 7 7 7 7 7 7 7 7 7 7 7 7
7 7 7 7 7 7 7 7 7 7 7 7 7 7 7 7 7 7 7 7 7 7 7 7 7 7 7 7 7 7 7 7 7 7 7
7 7 7 7 7 7 7 7 7 7 7 7 7 7 7 7 7 7 7 7 7 7 7 7 7 7 7 7 7 7 7 7 7 7 7
7 7 7 7 7 7 7 7 7 7 7 7 7 7 7 7 7 7 7 7 7 7 7 7 7 7 7 7 7 7 7 7 7 7 7
7 7 7 7 7 7 7 7 7 7 7 7 7 7 7 7 7 7 7 7 7 7 7 7 7 7 7 7 7 7 7 7 7 7 7
7 7 7 7 7 7 7 7 7 7 7 7 7 7 7 7 7 7 7 7 7 7 7 7 7 7 7 7 7 7 7 7 7 7 7
7 7 7 7 7 7 7 7 7 7 7 7 7 7 7 7 7 7 7 7 7 7 7 7 7 7 7 7 7 7 7 7 7 7 7
7 7 7 7 7 7 7 7 7 7 7 7 7 7 7 7 7 7 7 7 7 7 7 7 7 7 7 7 7 7 7 7 7 7 7

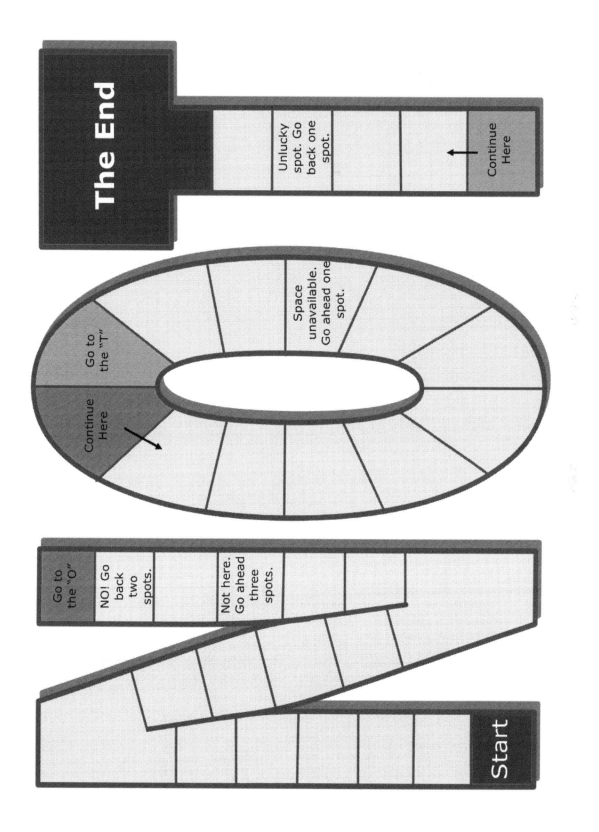

The End

Unlucky spot. Go back one spot.

Continue Here

Space unavailable. Go ahead one spot.

Go to the "T"

Continue Here

Go to the "O"

NO! Go back two spots.

Not here. Go ahead three spots.

Start

unlucky	unselfishly	unsuccessful	uncalled
unfair	unlimited	indecent	nonstop
unable	distracted	unscrewed	disinfecting
inevitable	discover	inattention	discredit
unlock	nonmetal	nonfiction	disagree

nonresident	nonelastic	nonprofit	nontoxic
inequality	infrequent	inexact	indirect
disfunction	disconnect	dismay	distrust
unmanned	unkind	unthinkable	uncontested
unfold	undo	unplug	unspoken

Player 1:
1

Player 2:
1

3 2 1 3 2 1

3 2 3 3 2 3

1 2 3 1 2 1

1 2 3 1 2 1

END

END

misspelled	misfit	subhuman	subway	reclaim	readjust
mishap	misrepresent	subtropical	subzero	refreshing	readjustment
misdirect	mistrust	subatomic	subdue	refresh	revisit
misprint	mismatch	subkingdom	subscript	react	redo
misled	misapply	subtotal	subsonic	retell	rerun
miscut	miscue	subplot	subclass	rewind	revisit

9 9 9 9 9 9 9 9 9 9 9 9 9 9 9 9 9 9 9 9 9 9 9 9 9 9 9 9 9 9
9 9 9 9 9 9 9 9 9 9 9 9 9 9 9 9 9 9 9 9 9 9 9 9 9 9 9 9 9 9
9 9 9 9 9 9 9 9 9 9 9 9 9 9 9 9 9 9 9 9 9 9 9 9 9 9 9 9 9 9
9 9 9 9 9 9 9 9 9 9 9 9 9 9 9 9 9 9 9 9 9 9 9 9 9 9 9 9 9 9
9 9 9 9 9 9 9 9 9 9 9 9 9 9 9 9 9 9 9 9 9 9 9 9 9 9 9 9 9 9
9 9 9 9 9 9 9 9 9 9 9 9 9 9 9 9 9 9 9 9 9 9 9 9 9 9 9 9 9 9
9 9 9 9 9 9 9 9 9 9 9 9 9 9 9 9 9 9 9 9 9 9 9 9 9 9 9 9 9 9
9 9 9 9 9 9 9 9 9 9 9 9 9 9 9 9 9 9 9 9 9 9 9 9 9 9 9 9 9 9
9 9 9 9 9 9 9 9 9 9 9 9 9 9 9 9 9 9 9 9 9 9 9 9 9 9 9 9 9 9
9 9 9 9 9 9 9 9 9 9 9 9 9 9 9 9 9 9 9 9 9 9 9 9 9 9 9 9 9 9
9 9 9 9 9 9 9 9 9 9 9 9 9 9 9 9 9 9 9 9 9 9 9 9 9 9 9 9 9 9
9 9 9 9 9 9 9 9 9 9 9 9 9 9 9 9 9 9 9 9 9 9 9 9 9 9 9 9 9 9
9 9 9 9 9 9 9 9 9 9 9 9 9 9 9 9 9 9 9 9 9 9 9 9 9 9 9 9 9 9
9 9 9 9 9 9 9 9 9 9 9 9 9 9 9 9 9 9 9 9 9 9 9 9 9 9 9 9 9 9
9 9 9 9 9 9 9 9 9 9 9 9 9 9 9 9 9 9 9 9 9 9 9 9 9 9 9 9 9 9
9 9 9 9 9 9 9 9 9 9 9 9 9 9 9 9 9 9 9 9 9 9 9 9 9 9 9 9 9 9
9 9 9 9 9 9 9 9 9 9 9 9 9 9 9 9 9 9 9 9 9 9 9 9 9 9 9 9 9 9
9 9 9 9 9 9 9 9 9 9 9 9 9 9 9 9 9 9 9 9 9 9 9 9 9 9 9 9 9 9
9 9 9 9 9 9 9 9 9 9 9 9 9 9 9 9 9 9 9 9 9 9 9 9 9 9 9 9 9 9
9 9 9 9 9 9 9 9 9 9 9 9 9 9 9 9 9 9 9 9 9 9 9 9 9 9 9 9 9 9
9 9 9 9 9 9 9 9 9 9 9 9 9 9 9 9 9 9 9 9 9 9 9 9 9 9 9 9 9 9
9 9 9 9 9 9 9 9 9 9 9 9 9 9 9 9 9 9 9 9 9 9 9 9 9 9 9 9 9 9
9 9 9 9 9 9 9 9 9 9 9 9 9 9 9 9 9 9 9 9 9 9 9 9 9 9 9 9 9 9
9 9 9 9 9 9 9 9 9 9 9 9 9 9 9 9 9 9 9 9 9 9 9 9 9 9 9 9 9 9
9 9 9 9 9 9 9 9 9 9 9 9 9 9 9 9 9 9 9 9 9 9 9 9 9 9 9 9 9 9
9 9 9 9 9 9 9 9 9 9 9 9 9 9 9 9 9 9 9 9 9 9 9 9 9 9 9 9 9 9
9 9 9 9 9 9 9 9 9 9 9 9 9 9 9 9 9 9 9 9 9 9 9 9 9 9 9 9 9 9
9 9 9 9 9 9 9 9 9 9 9 9 9 9 9 9 9 9 9 9 9 9 9 9 9 9 9 9 9 9
9 9 9 9 9 9 9 9 9 9 9 9 9 9 9 9 9 9 9 9 9 9 9 9 9 9 9 9 9 9
9 9 9 9 9 9 9 9 9 9 9 9 9 9 9 9 9 9 9 9 9 9 9 9 9 9 9 9 9 9

preexisting	preoccupy	subway	reclaim	submicroscopic	subcommittee
preexist	preoccupied	subzero	refreshing	predominantly	preoccupation
prepay	pretest	subdue	refresh	misrepresented	misapprehend
presoak	presold	preexist	misdirect	readjustment	reconstruction
preteen	preload	prepay	misprint	misrepresent	preeminent
prefix	prepacked	presoak	misled	precancellation	misconstruction

9 9 9 9 9 9 9 9 9 9 9 9 9 9 9 9 9 9 9 9 9 9 9 9 9 9 9 9 9 9 9 9 9
9 9 9 9 9 9 9 9 9 9 9 9 9 9 9 9 9 9 9 9 9 9 9 9 9 9 9 9 9 9 9 9 9
9 9 9 9 9 9 9 9 9 9 9 9 9 9 9 9 9 9 9 9 9 9 9 9 9 9 9 9 9 9 9 9 9
9 9 9 9 9 9 9 9 9 9 9 9 9 9 9 9 9 9 9 9 9 9 9 9 9 9 9 9 9 9 9 9 9
9 9 9 9 9 9 9 9 9 9 9 9 9 9 9 9 9 9 9 9 9 9 9 9 9 9 9 9 9 9 9 9 9
9 9 9 9 9 9 9 9 9 9 9 9 9 9 9 9 9 9 9 9 9 9 9 9 9 9 9 9 9 9 9 9 9
9 9 9 9 9 9 9 9 9 9 9 9 9 9 9 9 9 9 9 9 9 9 9 9 9 9 9 9 9 9 9 9 9
9 9 9 9 9 9 9 9 9 9 9 9 9 9 9 9 9 9 9 9 9 9 9 9 9 9 9 9 9 9 9 9 9
9 9 9 9 9 9 9 9 9 9 9 9 9 9 9 9 9 9 9 9 9 9 9 9 9 9 9 9 9 9 9 9 9
9 9 9 9 9 9 9 9 9 9 9 9 9 9 9 9 9 9 9 9 9 9 9 9 9 9 9 9 9 9 9 9 9
9 9 9 9 9 9 9 9 9 9 9 9 9 9 9 9 9 9 9 9 9 9 9 9 9 9 9 9 9 9 9 9 9
9 9 9 9 9 9 9 9 9 9 9 9 9 9 9 9 9 9 9 9 9 9 9 9 9 9 9 9 9 9 9 9 9
9 9 9 9 9 9 9 9 9 9 9 9 9 9 9 9 9 9 9 9 9 9 9 9 9 9 9 9 9 9 9 9 9
9 9 9 9 9 9 9 9 9 9 9 9 9 9 9 9 9 9 9 9 9 9 9 9 9 9 9 9 9 9 9 9 9
9 9 9 9 9 9 9 9 9 9 9 9 9 9 9 9 9 9 9 9 9 9 9 9 9 9 9 9 9 9 9 9 9
9 9 9 9 9 9 9 9 9 9 9 9 9 9 9 9 9 9 9 9 9 9 9 9 9 9 9 9 9 9 9 9 9
9 9 9 9 9 9 9 9 9 9 9 9 9 9 9 9 9 9 9 9 9 9 9 9 9 9 9 9 9 9 9 9 9
9 9 9 9 9 9 9 9 9 9 9 9 9 9 9 9 9 9 9 9 9 9 9 9 9 9 9 9 9 9 9 9 9
9 9 9 9 9 9 9 9 9 9 9 9 9 9 9 9 9 9 9 9 9 9 9 9 9 9 9 9 9 9 9 9 9
9 9 9 9 9 9 9 9 9 9 9 9 9 9 9 9 9 9 9 9 9 9 9 9 9 9 9 9 9 9 9 9 9
9 9 9 9 9 9 9 9 9 9 9 9 9 9 9 9 9 9 9 9 9 9 9 9 9 9 9 9 9 9 9 9 9
9 9 9 9 9 9 9 9 9 9 9 9 9 9 9 9 9 9 9 9 9 9 9 9 9 9 9 9 9 9 9 9 9
9 9 9 9 9 9 9 9 9 9 9 9 9 9 9 9 9 9 9 9 9 9 9 9 9 9 9 9 9 9 9 9 9
9 9 9 9 9 9 9 9 9 9 9 9 9 9 9 9 9 9 9 9 9 9 9 9 9 9 9 9 9 9 9 9 9
9 9 9 9 9 9 9 9 9 9 9 9 9 9 9 9 9 9 9 9 9 9 9 9 9 9 9 9 9 9 9 9 9
9 9 9 9 9 9 9 9 9 9 9 9 9 9 9 9 9 9 9 9 9 9 9 9 9 9 9 9 9 9 9 9 9
9 9 9 9 9 9 9 9 9 9 9 9 9 9 9 9 9 9 9 9 9 9 9 9 9 9 9 9 9 9 9 9 9
9 9 9 9 9 9 9 9 9 9 9 9 9 9 9 9 9 9 9 9 9 9 9 9 9 9 9 9 9 9 9 9 9
9 9 9 9 9 9 9 9 9 9 9 9 9 9 9 9 9 9 9 9 9 9 9 9 9 9 9 9 9 9 9 9 9
9 9 9 9 9 9 9 9 9 9 9 9 9 9 9 9 9 9 9 9 9 9 9 9 9 9 9 9 9 9 9 9 9
9 9 9 9 9 9 9 9 9 9 9 9 9 9 9 9 9 9 9 9 9 9 9 9 9 9 9 9 9 9 9 9 9
9 9 9 9 9 9 9 9 9 9 9 9 9 9 9 9 9 9 9 9 9 9 9 9 9 9 9 9 9 9 9 9 9
9 9 9 9 9 9 9 9 9 9 9 9 9 9 9 9 9 9 9 9 9 9 9 9 9 9 9 9 9 9 9 9 9
9 9 9 9 9 9 9 9 9 9 9 9 9 9 9 9 9 9 9 9 9 9 9 9 9 9 9 9 9 9 9 9 9

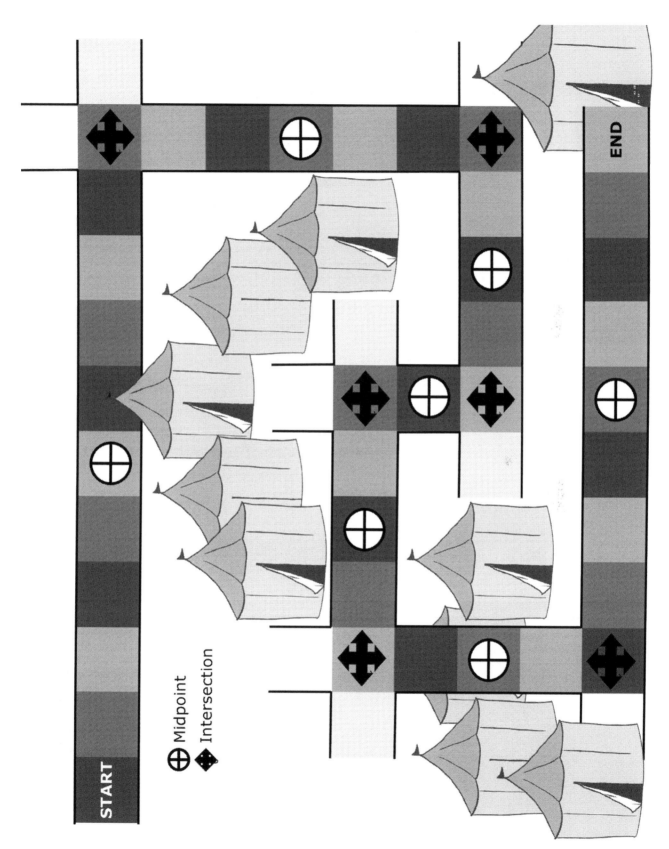

START

⊕ Midpoint

◆ Intersection

END

10 10 10 10 10 10 10 10 10 10 10 10 10 10 10 10 10 10
10 10 10 10 10 10 10 10 10 10 10 10 10 10 10 10 10 10
10 10 10 10 10 10 10 10 10 10 10 10 10 10 10 10 10 10
10 10 10 10 10 10 10 10 10 10 10 10 10 10 10 10 10 10
10 10 10 10 10 10 10 10 10 10 10 10 10 10 10 10 10 10
10 10 10 10 10 10 10 10 10 10 10 10 10 10 10 10 10 10
10 10 10 10 10 10 10 10 10 10 10 10 10 10 10 10 10 10
10 10 10 10 10 10 10 10 10 10 10 10 10 10 10 10 10 10
10 10 10 10 10 10 10 10 10 10 10 10 10 10 10 10 10 10
10 10 10 10 10 10 10 10 10 10 10 10 10 10 10 10 10 10
10 10 10 10 10 10 10 10 10 10 10 10 10 10 10 10 10 10
10 10 10 10 10 10 10 10 10 10 10 10 10 10 10 10 10 10
10 10 10 10 10 10 10 10 10 10 10 10 10 10 10 10 10 10
10 10 10 10 10 10 10 10 10 10 10 10 10 10 10 10 10 10
10 10 10 10 10 10 10 10 10 10 10 10 10 10 10 10 10 10
10 10 10 10 10 10 10 10 10 10 10 10 10 10 10 10 10 10
10 10 10 10 10 10 10 10 10 10 10 10 10 10 10 10 10 10
10 10 10 10 10 10 10 10 10 10 10 10 10 10 10 10 10 10
10 10 10 10 10 10 10 10 10 10 10 10 10 10 10 10 10 10
10 10 10 10 10 10 10 10 10 10 10 10 10 10 10 10 10 10
10 10 10 10 10 10 10 10 10 10 10 10 10 10 10 10 10 10
10 10 10 10 10 10 10 10 10 10 10 10 10 10 10 10 10 10
10 10 10 10 10 10 10 10 10 10 10 10 10 10 10 10 10 10
10 10 10 10 10 10 10 10 10 10 10 10 10 10 10 10 10 10
10 10 10 10 10 10 10 10 10 10 10 10 10 10 10 10 10 10
10 10 10 10 10 10 10 10 10 10 10 10 10 10 10 10 10 10
10 10 10 10 10 10 10 10 10 10 10 10 10 10 10 10 10 10
10 10 10 10 10 10 10 10 10 10 10 10 10 10 10 10 10 10
10 10 10 10 10 10 10 10 10 10 10 10 10 10 10 10 10 10
10 10 10 10 10 10 10 10 10 10 10 10 10 10 10 10 10 10
10 10 10 10 10 10 10 10 10 10 10 10 10 10 10 10 10 10
10 10 10 10 10 10 10 10 10 10 10 10 10 10 10 10 10 10
10 10 10 10 10 10 10 10 10 10 10 10 10 10 10 10 10 10

upset	oversee	interacted	midweek
upsetting	overreact	intersection	midday
upswing	overdue	interconnect	Midwest
uplift	overwhelmed	intermission	midbrain
upend	overlap	intermix	midway

10 10 10 10 10 10 10 10 10 10 10 10 10 10 10 10 10 10
10 10 10 10 10 10 10 10 10 10 10 10 10 10 10 10 10 10
10 10 10 10 10 10 10 10 10 10 10 10 10 10 10 10 10 10
10 10 10 10 10 10 10 10 10 10 10 10 10 10 10 10 10 10
10 10 10 10 10 10 10 10 10 10 10 10 10 10 10 10 10 10
10 10 10 10 10 10 10 10 10 10 10 10 10 10 10 10 10 10
10 10 10 10 10 10 10 10 10 10 10 10 10 10 10 10 10 10
10 10 10 10 10 10 10 10 10 10 10 10 10 10 10 10 10 10
10 10 10 10 10 10 10 10 10 10 10 10 10 10 10 10 10 10
10 10 10 10 10 10 10 10 10 10 10 10 10 10 10 10 10 10
10 10 10 10 10 10 10 10 10 10 10 10 10 10 10 10 10 10
10 10 10 10 10 10 10 10 10 10 10 10 10 10 10 10 10 10
10 10 10 10 10 10 10 10 10 10 10 10 10 10 10 10 10 10
10 10 10 10 10 10 10 10 10 10 10 10 10 10 10 10 10 10
10 10 10 10 10 10 10 10 10 10 10 10 10 10 10 10 10 10
10 10 10 10 10 10 10 10 10 10 10 10 10 10 10 10 10 10
10 10 10 10 10 10 10 10 10 10 10 10 10 10 10 10 10 10
10 10 10 10 10 10 10 10 10 10 10 10 10 10 10 10 10 10
10 10 10 10 10 10 10 10 10 10 10 10 10 10 10 10 10 10
10 10 10 10 10 10 10 10 10 10 10 10 10 10 10 10 10 10
10 10 10 10 10 10 10 10 10 10 10 10 10 10 10 10 10 10
10 10 10 10 10 10 10 10 10 10 10 10 10 10 10 10 10 10
10 10 10 10 10 10 10 10 10 10 10 10 10 10 10 10 10 10
10 10 10 10 10 10 10 10 10 10 10 10 10 10 10 10 10 10
10 10 10 10 10 10 10 10 10 10 10 10 10 10 10 10 10 10
10 10 10 10 10 10 10 10 10 10 10 10 10 10 10 10 10 10
10 10 10 10 10 10 10 10 10 10 10 10 10 10 10 10 10 10
10 10 10 10 10 10 10 10 10 10 10 10 10 10 10 10 10 10
10 10 10 10 10 10 10 10 10 10 10 10 10 10 10 10 10 10
10 10 10 10 10 10 10 10 10 10 10 10 10 10 10 10 10 10
10 10 10 10 10 10 10 10 10 10 10 10 10 10 10 10 10 10
10 10 10 10 10 10 10 10 10 10 10 10 10 10 10 10 10 10
10 10 10 10 10 10 10 10 10 10 10 10 10 10 10 10 10 10

uphill	upwind	uphold	upheld
upload	upsell	upshift	upstairs
updating	uplink	upbringing	upgrading
uploading	uplinking	uplifting	upper-class

10 10 10 10 10 10 10 10 10 10 10 10 10 10 10 10 10 10 10
10 10 10 10 10 10 10 10 10 10 10 10 10 10 10 10 10 10 10
10 10 10 10 10 10 10 10 10 10 10 10 10 10 10 10 10 10 10
10 10 10 10 10 10 10 10 10 10 10 10 10 10 10 10 10 10 10
10 10 10 10 10 10 10 10 10 10 10 10 10 10 10 10 10 10 10
10 10 10 10 10 10 10 10 10 10 10 10 10 10 10 10 10 10 10
10 10 10 10 10 10 10 10 10 10 10 10 10 10 10 10 10 10 10
10 10 10 10 10 10 10 10 10 10 10 10 10 10 10 10 10 10 10
10 10 10 10 10 10 10 10 10 10 10 10 10 10 10 10 10 10 10
10 10 10 10 10 10 10 10 10 10 10 10 10 10 10 10 10 10 10
10 10 10 10 10 10 10 10 10 10 10 10 10 10 10 10 10 10 10
10 10 10 10 10 10 10 10 10 10 10 10 10 10 10 10 10 10 10
10 10 10 10 10 10 10 10 10 10 10 10 10 10 10 10 10 10 10
10 10 10 10 10 10 10 10 10 10 10 10 10 10 10 10 10 10 10
10 10 10 10 10 10 10 10 10 10 10 10 10 10 10 10 10 10 10
10 10 10 10 10 10 10 10 10 10 10 10 10 10 10 10 10 10 10
10 10 10 10 10 10 10 10 10 10 10 10 10 10 10 10 10 10 10
10 10 10 10 10 10 10 10 10 10 10 10 10 10 10 10 10 10 10
10 10 10 10 10 10 10 10 10 10 10 10 10 10 10 10 10 10 10
10 10 10 10 10 10 10 10 10 10 10 10 10 10 10 10 10 10 10
10 10 10 10 10 10 10 10 10 10 10 10 10 10 10 10 10 10 10
10 10 10 10 10 10 10 10 10 10 10 10 10 10 10 10 10 10 10
10 10 10 10 10 10 10 10 10 10 10 10 10 10 10 10 10 10 10
10 10 10 10 10 10 10 10 10 10 10 10 10 10 10 10 10 10 10
10 10 10 10 10 10 10 10 10 10 10 10 10 10 10 10 10 10 10
10 10 10 10 10 10 10 10 10 10 10 10 10 10 10 10 10 10 10
10 10 10 10 10 10 10 10 10 10 10 10 10 10 10 10 10 10 10
10 10 10 10 10 10 10 10 10 10 10 10 10 10 10 10 10 10 10
10 10 10 10 10 10 10 10 10 10 10 10 10 10 10 10 10 10 10
10 10 10 10 10 10 10 10 10 10 10 10 10 10 10 10 10 10 10
10 10 10 10 10 10 10 10 10 10 10 10 10 10 10 10 10 10 10
10 10 10 10 10 10 10 10 10 10 10 10 10 10 10 10 10 10 10

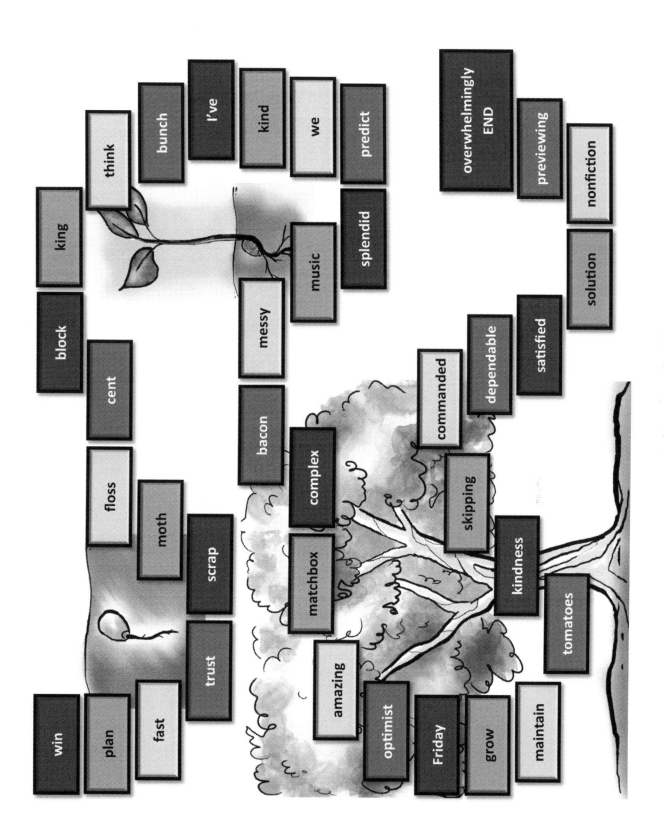

11 11 11 11 11 11 11 11 11 11 11 11 11 11 11 11
11 11 11 11 11 11 11 11 11 11 11 11 11 11 11 11
11 11 11 11 11 11 11 11 11 11 11 11 11 11 11 11
11 11 11 11 11 11 11 11 11 11 11 11 11 11 11 11
11 11 11 11 11 11 11 11 11 11 11 11 11 11 11 11
11 11 11 11 11 11 11 11 11 11 11 11 11 11 11 11
11 11 11 11 11 11 11 11 11 11 11 11 11 11 11 11
11 11 11 11 11 11 11 11 11 11 11 11 11 11 11 11
11 11 11 11 11 11 11 11 11 11 11 11 11 11 11 11
11 11 11 11 11 11 11 11 11 11 11 11 11 11 11 11
11 11 11 11 11 11 11 11 11 11 11 11 11 11 11 11
11 11 11 11 11 11 11 11 11 11 11 11 11 11 11 11
11 11 11 11 11 11 11 11 11 11 11 11 11 11 11 11
11 11 11 11 11 11 11 11 11 11 11 11 11 11 11 11
11 11 11 11 11 11 11 11 11 11 11 11 11 11 11 11
11 11 11 11 11 11 11 11 11 11 11 11 11 11 11 11
11 11 11 11 11 11 11 11 11 11 11 11 11 11 11 11
11 11 11 11 11 11 11 11 11 11 11 11 11 11 11 11
11 11 11 11 11 11 11 11 11 11 11 11 11 11 11 11
11 11 11 11 11 11 11 11 11 11 11 11 11 11 11 11
11 11 11 11 11 11 11 11 11 11 11 11 11 11 11 11
11 11 11 11 11 11 11 11 11 11 11 11 11 11 11 11
11 11 11 11 11 11 11 11 11 11 11 11 11 11 11 11
11 11 11 11 11 11 11 11 11 11 11 11 11 11 11 11
11 11 11 11 11 11 11 11 11 11 11 11 11 11 11 11
11 11 11 11 11 11 11 11 11 11 11 11 11 11 11 11
11 11 11 11 11 11 11 11 11 11 11 11 11 11 11 11
11 11 11 11 11 11 11 11 11 11 11 11 11 11 11 11
11 11 11 11 11 11 11 11 11 11 11 11 11 11 11 11
11 11 11 11 11 11 11 11 11 11 11 11 11 11 11 11
11 11 11 11 11 11 11 11 11 11 11 11 11 11 11 11
11 11 11 11 11 11 11 11 11 11 11 11 11 11 11 11
11 11 11 11 11 11 11 11 11 11 11 11 11 11 11 11